"I'm getting too carried away here, Jack,"

Mary said.

"So am I, but why fight it?"

"No, this kind of thing isn't me."

"Kissing isn't your kind of thing?" He gave her a skeptical smile.

Feeling herself turn red, she shook her head. "What I meant was, hot and heavy is not my style."

He trailed a finger down her bare arm. "Have you ever really given yourself the chance to find out?"

Dear Reader,

Welcome to Silhouette Special Edition…welcome to romance.

That telltale sign of falling leaves signals that autumn has arrived and so have heartwarming books to take you into the season.

Two exciting series from veteran authors continue in the month of September. Christine Rimmer's THE JONES GANG returns with *A Home for the Hunter*. And the Rogue River is once again the exciting setting for Laurie Paige's WILD RIVER series in *A River To Cross*.

This month, our THAT SPECIAL WOMAN! is Anna Louise Perkins, a courageous woman who rises to the challenge of bringing love and happiness to the man of her dreams. You'll meet her in award-winning author Sherryl Woods's *The Parson's Waiting*.

Also in September, don't miss *Rancher's Heaven* from Robin Elliott, *Miracle Child* by Kayla Daniels and *Family Connections*, a debut book in Silhouette Special Edition by author Judith Yates.

I hope you enjoy this book, and all of the stories to come!

Sincerely,

Tara Gavin
Senior Editor

Please address questions and book requests to:
Silhouette Reader Service
U.S.: 3010 Walden Ave., P.O. Box 1325, Buffalo, NY 14269
Canadian: P.O. Box 609, Fort Erie, Ont. L2A 5X3

JUDITH
YATES
FAMILY CONNECTIONS

Silhouette®

SPECIAL EDITION®

Published by Silhouette Books
America's Publisher of Contemporary Romance

To Margaret Iannacone, a wonderful aunt
and my number-one fan—
tell the coffee ladies I'll be up to sign their books.

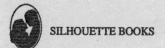

SILHOUETTE BOOKS

ISBN 0-373-09912-6

FAMILY CONNECTIONS

Copyright © 1994 by Judith Yoder

Printed in U.S.A.

JUDITH YATES

grew up in a tiny New England town where she secretly wrote novels after school. After such an early start, she finds it ironic that she didn't get around to "following her bliss" of writing professionally until after working for years in Boston and Washington, D.C., marrying and starting a family.

When she's not busy writing and taking care of her two small children, Judith volunteers at local schools and enjoys speaking to young people about writing—especially those who are secretly working on novels after school.

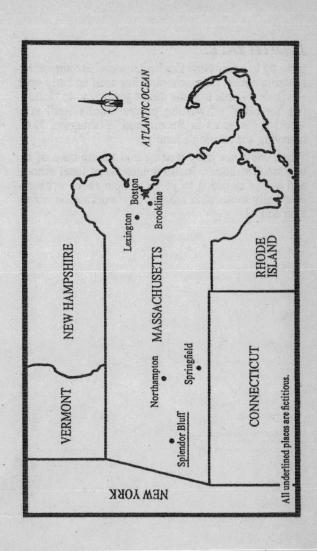

VERMONT

NEW HAMPSHIRE

MASSACHUSETTS

Splendor Bluff

Northampton

Springfield

Lexington

Boston

Brookline

ATLANTIC OCEAN

NEW YORK

CONNECTICUT

RHODE ISLAND

All underlined places are fictitious.

Chapter One

Mary Piletti heard the shouting the moment she drove into her parents' long driveway. The voices were loud, angry and male.

More wary than fearful, she strained to hear the argument. Even with the windows rolled down for relief from the August heat, she couldn't make out the words. As she pulled up to the house, however, she did recognize one of the participants in the shouting match. Peter Candelaria. What's he blowing off about now? she wondered. Her father's employee was usually butting heads with someone or another—but rarely during working hours, and never at the office adjoining her parents' house. Annoyed, she stopped the car within inches of the two men.

They didn't notice.

Mary got out of the car and then shoved herself between Peter Candelaria and his opponent. "What on earth's the matter with you, Peter?" she admonished, trying to keep from shouting herself. "You're going to upset my folks."

Her sudden intervention didn't faze him. "Relax, Mary. Your mother's out shopping," Peter said, his voice lower now, but still angry. "And Mario's taking a nap."

"Oh, great. We've probably woken him up," added a more restrained voice.

Mary spun around to face its owner. Dark brown eyes under a wave of rich dark hair stared down at her, intriguing despite the glint of lingering anger.

"Hello, Mary."

She tilted her head back to get a better look at this person who seemed to know her. A man of average height would be an apt description—except that was the only thing average about him. Her eyes skimmed across his trim, but by no means spare, physique before focusing on a face she thought rather attractive. And, she suddenly realized, familiar.

She shook off the notion and turned back to Peter. "You know my father needs his rest, and he's certainly not to be stressed in any way."

"I'm sorry, Mary, but this guy—"

"Does this have anything to do with the business, Peter?" She waved her arm at the one story addition on the side of the house. On its large front picture window the words Piletti Real Estate were painted in gold.

"No, it's him, and I—"

"Then take it elsewhere." Mary realized she sounded like she was scolding a third-grader, and she regretted resurrecting her teacher voice on a guy she'd known her whole life. Peter's wounded-puppy-dog look made her feel worse.

"Look, I'm sorry. But you can't have yelling matches with strangers in front of my parents' house."

"He's no stranger," Peter mumbled belligerently.

"Hardly," the man in question said, "but it is the nicest thing I've been called in the past fifteen minutes."

The man's sarcasm made her take another look. He really was a good-looking son of a gun, with his faded jeans molding just so to lean hips and powerful thighs, and a crisp navy blue T-shirt that might as well have I Work Out emblazoned across it. Full lips on an angular face and a tawny complexion gave a warm earthiness to his sharp features. Handsome and familiar. Vexingly so. But how could her memory be fuzzy about a man like this?

A knowing smile twinkled in his eyes, causing a pleasurable twinge in her chest.

"You don't remember me, Mary?"

Jack Candelaria, she thought, two full pulse beats passing before she managed to speak. "Of course. It's just you're the last person I'd expect to run into around here."

Jack's responding laugh had an edge to it as he nodded at his younger brother. "You and everyone else."

"I've had enough of you already, Jack." Peter backed away, yanking car keys from his pocket. "I don't know why you even bothered checking in with me. You're going to do whatever the hell you want, anyway. You always have.''

Mary felt sorry for Peter as he stomped off to his gray sedan. It seemed as if he couldn't get away from his brother fast enough, as if he felt the city of Springfield, Massachusetts, wasn't big enough for both of them. Which, to Mary's way of thinking, wasn't how it should be between brothers. She turned to Jack. ''Aren't you going to stop him?''

''No.''

''But he's upset.'' Peter made a careless three-point turn in front of them.

''Seems that way, doesn't it?''

Although she sensed the anger simmering beneath his words, it didn't stop her from speaking her mind. ''He's your brother. You should talk to him.''

His dark eyes narrowed. ''Now what would be the point?'' he asked, as Peter sped away. ''My brother has already decided I'm up to no good.''

''What are you up to?''

She could've bitten her tongue the moment she said it. Still, he was a neighborhood boy—or used to be. On close-knit Peek Street, this fact made polite curiosity, even blatant nosiness, acceptable. Everyone knew everyone else's business around here. Yet when she glanced up at him, his warm brown eyes had turned cool, reminding her that Jack Candelaria wasn't, and never had been, a typical neighborhood boy.

''Mary, you have a refreshing directness. Or is that a trait of Peek Street women I've forgotten?'' He didn't sound amused.

''How long have you been gone?''

"It's been almost twenty years since I left town. Three since I came back for Dad's funeral."

He said this with a matter-of-factness that seemed to disregard the enormous sadness his running away had caused the Candelarias. All the neighbors on Peek Street knew. Mary'd been only ten when Jack had left, but she still remembered Rose Candelaria's mournful tears, old Vito's bitterness and young Peter's bewilderment. Was Jack so unaware of how painful his long absence had been for his family? Did he care?

Or was he actually as selfish as the neighborhood wags had contended all these years?

"Mary, sweetheart! What was all that yelling about?" Her father pushed open the screen door, still flushed and rumpled from his afternoon nap.

Jack turned to the older man. "I'm sorry we woke you, Mr. Piletti. Things got out of hand and—"

"Out of hand," her father sputtered, holding on to the railing as he slowly sat down on the middle step. "That racket was loud enough to wake the dead, never mind a sleeping old man."

"Dad, are you all right?"

"I'm just fine, Mary," Mario replied, with that ever-so-slight tinge of irritation he used when he felt someone was acting overly concerned about his well-being. Mary thought of it as his "I'm not an invalid" voice. "Now where's Peter?" he continued. "I heard him, I know it."

"He left, Dad."

"What? He's supposed to be watching the office while Charlie's at a settlement this afternoon." Cursing in Italian under his breath, Mario shook his head. "What am I gonna do with that boy?"

Jack brushed past Mary to stand before her father. "He left because of me. I set him off, I'm afraid."

Her father looked up, squinting through gold-framed eyeglasses. "So my eyes aren't playing tricks— it is you."

"Mario." Jack held out his hand.

"Jackie—no, I should say Jack. You're a grown man now," her father said, getting to his feet to shake Jack's hand. "Tell me what's going on. Why's your brother upset with you this time?"

"I'm moving back to Springfield," Jack said quietly, as if such a simple announcement explained it all. "For good."

"I see," Mario murmured, exhibiting none of the shocked surprise Mary was feeling. Returning for good? After all these years? Mary wanted to ask why and half expected her father to do so. Instead he asked, "When?"

"I'm in the process. I'm going into business here."

Now her father did look surprised. "Doing what? Stockbroking? That's what you do in Boston, isn't it?"

"I was a broker," Jack said, a wry smile twitching his lips. "But not anymore. I've just bought the bicycle shop at the Twelve Trees shopping center. I'm going to run it."

"Ah, a bicycle shop." Mario studied the young man before him. "So you really mean to stay. Does your mama know this?"

"We've talked about it on the phone."

"She never said a word to us."

Again the fleeting trace of humor vanished from Jack's face. "Probably because she finds it as hard to believe as you do."

Her father calmly nodded. "It is something of a surprise."

Jack glanced over at Mary. "That's what I'm up to."

Before she had a chance to reply, he turned back to Mario. "I'm still winding up some business matters in Boston, and I'm selling my house there. For now I'm staying at a motel near Twelve Trees, but I'd like to find an apartment or house with a short-term lease. That's why I'm here," he added. "For some fool reason I thought my brother might help me find something."

"Never mind him. I'll help you," Mario offered.

Now it was Jack who seemed surprised. "Thank you, Mario. I really appreciate the trouble you're—"

Mario held up his hand to stop him. "Never mind that, either. Your father, God rest his soul, was my close friend."

"I know."

"Look, you go into the office and wait for me while I wash up," her father said. "Mary, honey, take Jack inside, okay?"

Not a word passed between them as she led Jack to the side entrance. Once inside the large air-conditioned office, she pointed to her father's desk and told Jack to have a seat. But he remained standing, his gaze fixed on the family photograph prominently displayed on the corner of the desk. He stared at it for several seconds until she asked him if he'd like a cold drink.

He shook his head and then finally looked up. "You and Charlie have stayed close to home. Like my brother."

She bristled. "Some of us had little choice."

From the flash of chagrin across his face, Mary realized Jack thought she meant his brother, when in actuality she was thinking about herself.

"Peter got stuck here because of me," he admitted. "I'm well aware of that—and other things."

"What other things?"

"Like moving back won't be easy. I committed the unpardonable crime to an Italian family—running away to pursue my own *selfish* dreams and—even worse—defying my father and breaking my mother's heart. For Peek Street, that's a lot to live down. Although I had no idea just how much of a pariah I've become around here." Shrugging, Jack stuck his hands in his jeans pockets. His bare forearms, lean and muscular under a dusting of dark hair, captured her attention. "But at least your father's giving me the benefit of the doubt. How about you?"

He came a step closer and she, unwittingly, took a step back. "I'm in no position to judge you."

"Maybe, maybe not. You were just a kid when I left." Jack leaned against her father's desk as his brown eyes roamed over her in slow, careful appraisal. "But you're all grown up now."

The expression in his eyes made her skin tingle with an electrified awareness, and suddenly she was self-conscious about how she looked and sounded and felt.

"What do you think, Mary? Am I just making trouble for everyone by coming back?"

His gaze held her pinned to the spot—there was no way she could squirm out of an answer. "It depends on your reasons, I guess. And what you're looking for."

"What if I told you what I told Peter? That I was looking for a more fulfilling way of life. Would you believe me?"

"I'd say it was understandable, considering..."

"Considering?"

"That you lost your wife last year. It's understandable that you'd want to escape painful reminders of—"

"Escaping 'painful reminders' has nothing do with it," he said brusquely, moving away from the desk. "I'm coming home because I belong here, plain and simple."

Mary sensed it was anything but plain and simple. Yet Jack's strong reaction left her at a loss for words, and she was relieved her father rejoined them then. As the two men settled down to business, she went into the house, wondering if it'd been insensitive of her to mention Jack's late wife. Obviously she had touched a nerve. His reaction, however, was not voiced with sorrow or grief as one might expect. No, Jack spoke with an underlying bitterness she found puzzling—and disturbing.

Disturbing in more ways than one, she mused, recalling how his gaze made her feel. Well, attraction was easy enough to brush aside. But there was more to what she was feeling now than just that. Her curiosity was aroused. The very nature of his return to Springfield—sudden, unapologetic, almost defiant really—was intriguing. Jack Candelaria was different—quite different—from the men she'd grown up with. She had a feeling that if Jack settled here as he planned, the old neighborhood wouldn't ever be quite the same.

"Mary?"

"In the kitchen," she called to her brother, Charlie.

"I just got back and was out in the office," he said, plunking himself down at the kitchen table. "I can't believe Jack Candelaria's here."

"Strange, isn't it?"

"And he's bought a bicycle shop? I thought he was a stockbroker."

Mary pulled a pitcher of ice tea from the refrigerator. "Any idea what that's about?"

"He used to be big into bicycle racing, back when we were in high school."

"I didn't know that." She poured tea into two tall glasses.

"In fact, I think he joined the racing circuit right after he left. Toured quite a bit over in Europe early on. At least that's what I heard."

Mary could just see Jack Candelaria, strong shoulders hunched over handlebars, his taut legs pedaling forcefully as he raced through the French countryside. What adventures he must've had, she mused as she sat down. But she pushed envy aside and turned to Charlie. "Peter's fit to be tied." She then explained about the scene in front of the house.

"Great, just what he needs—a bigger chip on his shoulder. He's an old friend, but sometimes..." Letting the thought drift off, Charlie took a long sip of tea. Then he gave her a speculative look over the rim of his glass. "What are you doing here, anyway? I thought you were staying in Hartford until tomorrow."

"I didn't feel like staying for the banquet, so I cut out after the last seminar," she explained. "Besides, I have several huge bags of clothes at my place that I have to inspect and tag by Monday. I can't fall behind on these back-to-school consignments." She knew that more fall items would be arriving daily at her shop, Twice as Nice, and already a handful of her loyal clientele had been calling to get a first peek at her latest stock of quality used children's clothing. Late summer was always her busiest time.

"So, how was the conference?" Charlie asked.

The enthusiasm that was lost during the earlier ruckus returned with a rush. She gave her older brother a big smile. "Actually, pretty fruitful. I met with the Michael sisters, and a partnership may be in the offing," she revealed. "We agreed the demand for quality used children's clothing in the Boston suburbs is strong—strong enough to support several outlets, since the population there is more transient. If it works out, I'll have to move to Boston."

Charlie tapped his fingers against his glass. "A fact that doesn't displease you at all."

"I've been wanting to strike out on my own for years. You know that."

"You have been on your own since the day you moved out of this house."

"Self-supporting—for the most part. But autonomous? Independent?" She shook her head. "The family ties have been too secure for that."

"Ah, come on, Mary. You make it sound like the family's forcibly handcuffed you to Springfield."

Never forcibly, she thought wryly. Yet the emotional restraints of duty, responsibility and love were strong—strong enough for her to force herself to stay those times she'd been ready to leave. Mary knew it was pointless to argue this with Charlie. With a wife and two young kids, he was all settled in a large, lovely house less than a mile away, and the family real estate business was his now. His satisfaction, his happiness was right here in Springfield. Mary couldn't say the same for herself. Oh, she was content, and certainly her business was profitable, but it wasn't enough. She expected more, *wanted* more, from life.

"Hey! Aren't you happy for me?" she asked.

Charlie sighed. "Sure I'm happy for you, Mare. But if, for some reason, the partnership doesn't work out, you can still expand in this area. There are worse things than staying in Springfield."

"I know," she agreed, although she knew her voice lacked conviction. It wasn't that she considered her hometown a dead end, but after living there her entire life, she yearned for the challenge of something new. Finally, on her thirtieth birthday, years of feeling adrift had caught up with her. She knew then, without a doubt, that her fulfillment had to be found elsewhere.

"Hey, it's good enough for even Jack Candelaria to come back. Just think, you two have something in common—you're both Springfield small-business owners."

Mary grimaced before swallowing the last of her ice tea as another thought occurred to her. She put her empty glass down. "Charlie, did Peter ever say anything to you about the woman Jack married?"

"Only after she was killed in that car crash," Charlie explained. "And that was to ask for the day off to drive his mother to the funeral in Boston. Why?"

She shrugged. "No reason, really. Except Jack never brought her here, not even for his father's funeral. Seems strange, doesn't it?"

"Who's to say? Vito Candelaria, stubborn old fool that he was, didn't go to Jack's wedding, and you know why?"

"Because they were being married by a judge, or something like that, I think. Or was it because the bride wasn't Italian?"

Charlie shook his head. "Peter claims the family wasn't invited."

Leaning back in her chair, Mary combed a hand through her dark shoulder-length hair, now slightly frizzed from the humidity. *What is it with the men in that family?* she wondered. Their passionate temperaments had to make life difficult for those close to them. True, her own family had their emotional moments, but the Candelarias played their lives out on a different plane altogether. Every conflict was a major drama in which anyone in close vicinity became a captive. It happened to her today, when by accident she came upon Peter and Jack fighting.

Mary had no patience for that, especially now that she was finally free to go after what she wanted. Unlike Charlie, who was friends with Peter, and unlike her mother, who was close to Rose, the Candelarias' problems wouldn't—couldn't—become her own.

Besides, she was feeling very positive about the Michael sisters and the partnership, and her hunches were usually good. If all went as hoped, she'd be embarking on a new life. Thank goodness she'd be too far away to be dragged into the Candelaria family quarrels.

Charlie left to track Peter down, so Mary rinsed out their glasses and tidied up the kitchen a bit while she waited for her mother to return. Just after she sat down with one of her mother's women's magazines, her father came bustling in. Jack was right behind him.

"Oh, Mary, you're still here. Good," her father declared as he waved what looked to be a rental agreement in front of her face. "I need a favor."

Wariness crept over her. "Yes?"

"I rented 3-B to Jack. Could you give him a ride over there? His car's in the shop."

Three-B was the only vacant apartment in the six-unit building her father owned and which she managed for some additional income.

She also lived in that building.

"But we're keeping 3-B vacant until we refurbish it entirely." The previous tenants had literally turned the apartment into a battlefield for their own bitter divorce war. The couple had done some heavy damage before she was able to evict them. Mary looked up at Jack. "The place is a mess."

"So I understand."

"Jack only needs it for two or three months, until I help him find a house to buy," Mario interjected. "He's offered to do the work on the apartment in exchange for a month-to-month lease."

"He has?" She wasn't thrilled about this unexpected turn of events, although she wasn't sure why. Again she peered up at Jack. "We're not talking about a simple cleaning and paint job, you know."

"Mary," her father barked, "I told him."

"Mario's been up-front about the apartment's condition," Jack said, his tone so even she wasn't sure if her objection had irked him or not. "For the time being it suits my needs."

"But all that work—"

"I put myself through college by working on construction jobs, so I know what I'm doing. Besides, I like working with my hands."

Almost as if they had a shameless mind of their own, her eyes sought his hands. His fingers were long and straight. And the masculine patch of black hair on the back of each hand had her wondering if they felt as strong as they looked. Then Mary realized what she was doing.

Averting her gaze, she got to her feet and took the rental agreement from her father. She realized she was uncomfortable with the idea of Jack living in her building. She just wasn't sure why. Was she wary of his reputation? After all, Jack was not a popular guy around this neighborhood. Perhaps she feared being swept up in the Candelaria's family strife—the angry fight she broke up between the two brothers would make anyone leery. Whatever the reason, her intuition was sounding the alarm: Trouble. And her intuition often proved to be correct.

"Jack, before we make it official, I think it's only fair you see the apartment for yourself. Dad may not realize just how bad it is."

"Mary!"

"It isn't necessary," Jack said calmly.

"But I insist." She reached for her handbag on the kitchen counter. "I'll take you over right now."

Chapter Two

"So, Mary, why don't you want me to rent the apartment?" Jack asked as Mary turned right on Peek Street.

Startled hazel eyes glanced over at him before quickly returning to the road. "I told you why."

"I don't buy that," he said, shaking his head. "Have you decided you are in a position to judge me, after all?"

"The place is a mess, Jack." She kept her gaze glued to the steady traffic. "Besides, it really doesn't matter what I think about your coming back, does it?"

Jack shrugged without answering and then stared out the passenger window. No, it didn't matter what she thought about it. When he'd decided to move back, he'd figured there would be opposition from his brother as well as disapproval from those Peek Street neighbors with unforgiving memories. They weren't going to deter him from doing what he wanted, however, and neither, of all people, was Mary Piletti.

Turning to Mary again, he studied her profile from across the front seat. Brown hair fell straight from a feathery fringe of bangs and grazed her shoulders like a thick dark veil. With its glints of summer sun gold, Mary's hair softened her strong features—features neither pert nor pretty, but striking. Very, very striking.

He had to admit it. He found this woman in the cool white suit very attractive. And he had since the moment she'd wedged her curvy body between his and Peter's while trying to stop their argument. Yet there was something more, something that had nothing to do with a pleasing face and a luscious figure. But what? The concerned look in her eyes when Peter ran off? Or the gentleness of her voice when she mentioned his late wife?

"I gather you've heard talk about me over the years," he said, still gazing at her. What she thought of him didn't matter, either, yet he wanted to know.

"It's been hard to avoid."

He shook his head. "You'd think people would forget."

"Forgetting comes after forgiving, I believe," she declared calmly. "Maybe if you'd tried to mend some fences over the past twenty years or so, people around here might be more receptive now."

Hmm. Miss Mary might not be as sympathetic to him as he'd first thought. Well, it wasn't the first time he'd misjudged a woman. "Look, Mary, I'm not about to ask Peek Street to forgive me for the way I've conducted my life," he declared, as the car pulled into the small parking lot behind a three-story brick building.

She parked the compact in a space marked Reserved and turned off the ignition. "Do you need to?" she asked, with an expression so inexplicably stern, he was reminded of Sister Mary Carlotta, his fifth-grade teacher at St. Anthony's.

"Are you a schoolteacher?" He had to ask.

A whisper of a smile softened her face. "Used to be."

Jack laughed as he pushed open the car door. "Thought so." He started walking toward the apartment building.

"Hey, you didn't answer the question," Mary called after him as she locked the car.

"Do I need to ask for forgiveness?" he repeated, while reassessing Mary's directness. It could turn out to be a royal pain. "You know, Mary, I think I'm in no position to judge."

Thankfully she let it go at that and led him inside the building. The halls were painted regulation white, unadorned but clean. The sturdy industrial wall-to-wall carpeting looked freshly vacuumed. It appeared Mary took good care of the place.

"Three-B's on the third floor, of course." She started up the first flight of stairs. "Sorry, there's no elevator."

"No problem."

She glanced back at him, her eyes traveling from head to toe. "I guess not."

No prim schoolteacher, she, Jack mused, stifling a grin as he followed her up. Yet this time, oddly enough, he appreciated Mary's directness. She may not think highly of him, but she was no game player, either—which suited him just fine. After years of rat-race double-talk, he preferred his dealings with people to be straightforward, honest. Well, as honest as he or anyone could afford to be.

Right now he honestly liked following her up three flights of stairs. Her round bottom moved softly under her white knit skirt as she climbed, tantalizing him with thoughts and images that had long been absent from his mind.

Okay, so Mary was attractive. But he wasn't crazy. He had come back to Springfield with an agenda for straightening out his life. Dallying with a Peek Street girl, especially the daughter of his family's closest friends, was not on his list. And for good reason.

Finally they reached 3-B and he followed her inside. "See what I mean?" she said, slightly out of breath from the long climb up.

Jack took it all in: chipped plaster, coffee-splattered walls, cracked windowpanes, broken light fixtures, torn wallpaper. The kitchen was filthy, with grease-coated fixtures, a dented refrigerator door, missing stove burners, and the bathroom was more of the same. It was worse than he'd imagined.

He shook his head. "No offense, Mary, but how could you let them get away with this? I mean, I can see how well maintained the rest of the building is."

"Believe me, I would've put a stop to it at the first sign of trouble. Except the first sign didn't come until it was too late."

"Didn't the other tenants realize what was going on?"

"We all work during the day, but the Fillmores—the couple who lived here—had night jobs. Apparently all the big fights happened during the day when no one was around. At night, when we were home, they were gone," she explained. "No yelling, no noise, nothing.

"Then last week, Mr. Ponzini in 2-A stayed home from work with the flu. The Fillmores started in on one doozy of a fight, so he called the police and me." She waved her hand over the mess. "This is what we found."

"Hope you kept a sizable security deposit."

She fought a smile. "I did that much right."

He took another look around. "I'll take it."

"What?"

"Did you bring the rental agreement in with you?"

"Jack, surely you don't want to bother with all this."

"It's mostly cosmetic stuff that needs to be done—nothing I can't handle."

"Are you serious?"

"Look, Mary, I'm sick of living in a motel. And I don't have a hell of a lot of patience with driving all over town looking for a place that'll give me a short-term lease. Especially when I have to find a house to buy so I don't lose my shirt in taxes." He supposed he sounded terse, but he disliked having to explain himself.

She didn't look convinced. "Yet you have the patience to fix this place up?"

"I told you, I like to work with my hands." That was true. He found it relaxing. Rehabbing the old house back in Lexington had saved his sanity after too many stressful days at the office. It also had kept him occupied on the countless nights he'd made it home from work but Sandra hadn't.

"It's your decision," she said, pulling the rental agreement from her oversize handbag. "I have a cleaning crew scheduled for Monday morning."

"Great. I'll move my things in Monday night." He signed the agreement and handed it back to her. "I may need help with the electric appliances."

"Let me know. I'll call a repairman." Her voice was tinged with resignation. "Of course we'll reimburse you for the materials you buy."

"Thanks," he replied. "Now if I can use your phone to call a cab, I'll be on my way."

Downstairs in her apartment, Jack walked into a living room scattered with trash-can-size plastic bags and cardboard boxes stuffed full with—he lifted a tiny garment from one of them. "Baby clothes?" he asked, as he held the formless nightgown in the air.

"Inventory. Infants and kids clothes up to size fourteen." Mary picked up two heavy bags and moved them out of the way. "Except I carry very little in the larger sizes. Older kids are picky, they only want the very latest styles."

He was still stuck on inventory. "What business are you in?"

"Used children's clothing, toys, baby equipment— mostly consignments. I have a shop off Chestnut Street."

"Is there that much demand for this stuff?" he asked, mystified. Children played virtually no part in his life. Although he and Sandra had planned to have a family when they were first married, they'd become too involved with their careers to make time and space in their lives for children. He'd been regretting that a lot lately.

"Enough demand for me to make a reasonable living. A lot of young mothers live far from their families, so hand-me-downs are difficult to come by," she explained. "And good quality kids' clothes are very expensive these days. Some mothers sell outgrown outfits through me, and with their profit buy larger ones for their children. I've been in business three years, and sales increase each year." She removed a box of clothes from the coffee table. "I substitute teach occasionally, and I manage this building for Dad. So I get by."

A few pint-size T-shirts were folded neatly on the end table. Jack moved them away from the telephone, a tad disconcerted by their sheer smallness. "Certainly is an interesting form of recycling."

"That, too," she said, and laughed.

He liked the sound of it—vibrant, guileless and a tad husky. This sexy laugh and the smoky hue of her eyes as she gazed at him warmed him, yet still added to his general wariness.

"The phone book's under there," she said, pointing to the sofa.

"Right," he said, finally turning away from her to fetch the phone book.

He dialed the first cab company listed and immediately was put on hold. But waiting gave him the opportunity to watch Mary as she moved about the room. He had no qualms about partaking in that harmless pleasure. Besides, he'd always been a sucker for a great pair of legs, and hers were lovely, lithe accents to her womanly curves.

A stirring low in his body rolled sharply though him. It'd been so long since he'd felt this way, since he'd felt anything, period. He savored the sensation by taking a long, deep breath and then let it go. Don't get sidetracked, he told himself. The idea in coming back had been to simplify life, not complicate it.

He wished to hell someone at that cab company would pick up the line and rescue him from "hold." Thoughts of Mary sleeping a mere two flights of stairs away from him every night filled his head, making him uneasy. She'd be too damn close for comfort. And too far away....

Mary pulled into her parking space, glad to be home after a hectic, but good, Saturday at Twice as Nice. The shop had been buzzing with moms—some with kids in tow—who were getting an early start on back-to-school shopping. Also, a surprising number of new mothers had popped into the shop today. They were attracted by her extensive selection of infant clothing—adorable outfits worn once or twice before being outgrown. These customers were her favorites, especially when they came with their sweet babies bundled snugly against their chests or in back carriers.

Sales had been good today, she thought happily, as she yanked a bag of newly received clothes from the back seat. She was planning to inspect and tag them tonight after supper and a hot bath. Maybe she'd even treat herself to a glass of wine to celebrate the phone call she received this morning from Lorna and Terry

Michael. They definitely wanted to get together to talk details about a new venture.

Yes, this had been a good day.

"Hi-ya, Mary. Can I carry that for ya?" Lou Ponzini from apartment 2-A walked up to her car.

She gathered Lou was just returning from his daily power walk, since he was wearing colorful coordinated shorts and T-shirt, as well as the latest in expensive walking shoes. His bald head was shiny with sweat.

"Don't you usually exercise in the morning?" she asked, handing him the heavy plastic bag.

"Yeah, but I got in pretty late last night." He gave a conspiratorial wink as they approached the building. "I'm seeing a widow out in Longmeadow and I—what the—?"

Loud arguing seeped down from third-story windows, and Mary recognized the two voices at once. "Not again."

Lou nodded. "Sounds like the Fillmores all over again. What is it about 3-B?"

"I wish I knew, Lou," she said with a sigh, caught somewhere between wariness and annoyance. "I wish I knew."

"Maybe I should go speak to them," Lou offered, "before things get out of hand."

"No, I'll go." She wasn't eager to, but it was her job to keep order in the building.

"Not alone."

"It's okay, Lou, really." She unlocked the front door for them both. "I grew up with Peter Candelaria. He's all bark and no bite."

His older brother is another story, she added silently, uneasy about confronting Jack. She hadn't seen him since he moved in earlier in the week. But she'd thought about him—thought about him a lot.

Rushing up the three flights of stairs made her skin feel flushed and sticky. The odor of wet paint filled her nostrils as she stopped in the corridor to catch her breath. She saw that the door to 3-B was half-open, and the voices grew louder, more strident. But once Mary realized what they were fighting about, anger overran her awkwardness. No way would she allow the Candelarias' domestic drama to disturb the peace of her building.

Without bothering to knock, she swung open the door. "Peter—Jack—stop this right now!" she shouted loudly, so loudly she scared herself. Yet it was enough to quiet them. "Don't you two have anything better to do than fight like a pair of eight-year-olds?"

Peter glared at her. "And don't you have anything better to do than butt into other people's business all the time?"

"It is my business when it happens here. And unless you calm down, you'll have to leave."

Peter swore, raising his arms in the air as if in surrender. "I'm outta here, Mary." He brushed past her, slamming the door behind him.

Jack let out a low whistle. "You must've kept your students quaking in their sneakers."

"In the classroom a teacher's nothing without discipline," she said, finally looking at him. Wearing only a pair of black cotton shorts, Jack looked as sexy as all get-out. His tanned skin glistened with perspiration and an occasional splatter of off-white paint.

His broad shoulders and muscular chest were in striking proportion: lean, strong, hard—beautiful really—not unlike the age-old sculptures she'd seen in Florence and Rome. As Mary's gaze traveled along the narrow spread of dark hair from his chest down to his tapering waist, a chain of shivers taunted her spine and she had to look away.

"Right now I wish I could maintain some discipline in this apartment," she managed to mutter at last. "First the Fillmores, now you." The air in the room was stifling, so she moved a step closer to the box fan humming furiously on the floor. The breeze cooled her legs, but didn't—couldn't—do a thing for the heat of attraction simmering within her.

"I apologize for this, um, altercation," Jack said, sounding annoyed as he moved an open can of paint out of his path.

"Can't you two come to some sort of truce?"

"I'd be delighted to. But as you saw and heard, my brother is incapable of having a civil conversation with me." He reached for the red bandanna hanging from his back pocket, using it to wipe his damp forehead. "Actually, he doesn't want to have anything to do with me."

"Then why was he here?"

"You don't beat around the bush, do you?" He glared at her for a moment and then shrugged his shoulders. "To tell me to turn down my mother's invitation to supper tonight."

"And are you?"

"You're nosy, too," he added with a shake of his head. But she noticed he was trying not to smile. "I'm going, of course. Ma is truly glad I've come home, and she has her heart set on getting us together. Besides, it's still as much her house as his."

"Sounds like it's going to be a fun evening," she quipped. "Are you sure you want to put yourself—and your mother—through it?"

She was surprised by the flicker of doubt in his deep brown eyes. "Have to start somewhere, don't we?"

"I guess so."

Jack frowned and turned away, as if her response somehow disappointed him. Oddly enough, Mary felt a pang of sympathy for him then, making her wish she could think of something wise or philosophical or even comforting to say. Yet how could she, when she wasn't sure what to make of his situation or of him?

He rummaged through a pile of books and clothes and found a white T-shirt. Mary watched his back muscles flex as he yanked it over his head and stretched the smooth cotton over his shoulders. She breathed in deeply, entranced by the masculine grace of each movement. Good Lord, she thought ruefully, she was so attracted to this man.

Jack offered her a cold drink, which she declined before making her excuses to leave. "Wait, Mary," he said when she moved toward the door. He pulled a drop cloth off a blond wood armchair and invited her to sit, with a silent wave of his arm. "Please," he added when she hesitated.

Although reluctant on many counts about staying, Mary sat down. She was, after all, curious.

"Look, I understand why Peter is bitter," Jack began, resting his arm on the top step of a paint-splattered stepladder. "He's the one who stayed here all these years, helping my father with the store until it went out of business. And as our parents have gotten older, he's the one who's been responsible for them."

"Because you've never been around," Mary added pointedly, feeling a certain loyalty to the recalcitrant Peter.

"Yes, of course." His voice was as crisp as his stare. "But he uses his resentment of me as an excuse for his failings."

She couldn't believe what she was hearing. "An excuse?"

"For not finishing college. For marrying too young. And for working most of his adult life for your father, when I'm sure he'd hoped for something more. He blames me because he's discontent, but it was and is up to him to make the most of his life, regardless."

"Regardless of anyone or anything else?" Mary knew how accusing this sounded, but Jack had hit a nerve. What arrogance he had. "Maybe, like most people, Peter can't operate that way."

"Unlike me?"

"Take it any way you want," she said with a shrug. "But I can understand some of Peter's frustration. Look, I'm thirty years old and I never thought I'd still be here in Springfield at this point in my life. I've had plans.... Things happen, though, dreams get waylaid."

"By choice or circumstance?"

The question threw her, and she looked at him in surprise. "Maybe both."

She could tell that Jack was expecting more, that her simple answer didn't satisfy him. Yet she didn't feel comfortable enough to explain, especially to a man who, as far as she knew, had never made a sacrifice for anyone in his life.

To her relief he didn't ask.

They sat in silence for a while, Mary gazing down at her hands, feeling Jack's contemplative gaze still on her. She realized she should get up and leave, because clearly they didn't have anything else to say to each other. But having this handsome brown-eyed man looking at her like that thrilled her deep inside. She couldn't budge for wondering what was on his mind. Was he put off by her forthrightness? Did he think of her just as the girl who used to live down the street or as a grown woman? Did he find her attractive?

"Mary?"

"Yes?" She jerked her head up, feeling herself blush with needless embarrassment. He couldn't know what she'd been thinking.

"Perhaps you could help me and my family by coming to supper tonight."

"What?"

"Don't you see?" he said, moving away from the ladder. "A third party might take the heat off everyone. Make things less intense. If we can get together this first time without bickering, well..."

"What makes you think my presence will help? I suspect I'm not Peter's favorite person these days."

"With both my mother and you at the table, he'll behave." Then he grinned. "After all, you are his boss's daughter."

"That's never made a difference before," she remarked. "Besides, I wasn't invited. I can't intrude."

"I'll call and ask Ma. She'll be thrilled." Jack lowered himself in front of her chair, his face now level with hers. "She'll be comfortable with you."

She was sorry Rose was caught between her two warring sons, especially now that one had finally come home. Mary liked Jack's mother a great deal and wouldn't mind helping her out. If spending a couple of hours at the Candelarias' would keep everyone calm, well, why not? And if this dinner started Jack and Peter on the road to making up, then she wouldn't have to worry about loud fights here in the apartment building or at her parents' place. She hoped.

"I'm doing this for Rose," she insisted. "And I don't want your family to get the wrong idea about us."

"Wrong idea? You mean that you and I...?" Quickly his puzzled expression turned cool. "Not a chance, Mary. They know you're smarter than that."

His icy tone made her wince. She hadn't meant to offend him, and she felt foolish for even voicing the concern. After they settled on a time to meet, she hurried out of there, filled with second thoughts. It's for Rose, she kept reminding herself, as she made her way downstairs. Yet when she reached the second floor she stopped, struck by the annoying realization that she'd been sucked smack dab into the middle of that family's troubles.

The Candelarias had struck again.

Chapter Three

Jack was glad Mary was by his side tonight.

This was an important night for him. Getting together with his family for supper meant a first step toward reconciliation and another step toward the new life he wanted to make here in Springfield. It was nice to have an ally, albeit a reluctant one, facing it with him.

As they walked the three blocks to his mother's house—Peter's house now—his apprehension was ebbing with the warm evening breeze. Even Mary appeared calmer than he would've expected, and she looked great. Graceful and supple in a lemon yellow sundress, she looked cool yet touchable—enticingly touchable. And how he itched to touch her, to skim his hand along her smooth arm, perhaps sliding the delicate yellow strap off her creamy shoulder and slipping his hand down to her soft, full breasts. The fantasy sparked a shudder of excitement that he concentrated hard to suppress.

Jack forced himself to visualize Mary as the skinny-kneed little girl with pigtails and braces he'd known twenty years ago. Otherwise his resolve to keep her at arm's length would be in jeopardy. He didn't want or need that kind of distraction at this point.

Why was he worrying, anyway? Mary didn't even like him.

"Well, here we are," she said, when they reached the house.

He took a deep breath. "Yep, here we are."

"Good luck."

"Thanks." He pressed the doorbell. "I'm gonna need it."

Peter's wife, Gina, let them in with a stiff welcome, scarcely hiding the awkwardness she and everyone else was feeling. But Jack took her swift peck on his cheek as a hopeful sign. She embraced Mary with obvious relief. "Ma's so glad you're joining us."

Ma's not the only one, Jack thought wryly.

"Why don't you two go ahead to the living room, and I'll get Ma. Oh, Peter's in there with Aunt Angie," Gina added before disappearing into the kitchen—in a hurry.

Mary stopped short, glaring up at him. "You didn't tell me your Aunt Angie was going to be here."

"I didn't know," he answered, understanding her panic. Aunt Angie blamed him for every and any misfortune that had befallen the Candelaria family during the past twenty years—especially the demise of the family business: Candy's Neighborhood Grocery.

And she would never, ever forgive him. Which Mary knew. Damn, the entire neighborhood knew.

Mary shook her head. "This isn't going to work, Jack."

Fearing she was about to walk out, he took her hand and appealed directly to her pensive gold-green eyes. "Don't bail out on me now. Please."

"Jackie—Mary," his mother cried with pleasure as she burst into the hallway, "welcome, welcome." Rose took one look at their clasped hands and suddenly her face beamed with approval. One didn't have to be clairvoyant to figure what she was thinking.

Mary dropped his hand fast.

"Ma, what's Aunt Angie doing here? Didn't she know I was coming?"

"I didn't invite her." Scowling, Rose shook her head. "She got wind you'd be here, so she just showed up—to cause trouble, no doubt."

Jack knew his mother wouldn't be able to turn his father's elder sister away. She was family; it just wasn't done. "Please, Jackie, stay calm—for my sake," Rose urged. "Don't let Angie bait you into arguing. That's what she wants."

He followed his mother and Mary into the living room where Angie Candelaria, unyielding and indomitable, sat waiting on the sofa.

By the time everyone was finished eating roast chicken and Rose's wonderful manicotti, Mary was ready to scream. Six adults, two children and a baby sat at the dining room table awaiting an explosion. Out of sheer anxiety, she had eaten a third helping of the pasta and drunk a second glass of wine.

From the moment she and Jack had entered the living room, Angie Candelaria had simply refused to acknowledge Jack's presence. She had engaged everyone in conversation except him. When Mary or Rose tried to include him, Angie would pointedly exclude him. Naturally all the Candelarias were too respectful of Angie's age and position in the family to call her on such rude behavior. Mary had forced herself to hold her tongue a time or two as well.

The dinner table was worse. Peter, sullen, barely spoke. Gina, busy settling down their two boys and feeding the baby, said even less. But she seemed to be annoyed with Peter about something. And although Rose and Jack tried their best to keep a cheerful conversation going, good old Angie grabbed every opportunity to lament the loss of the family's grocery business. How hard Vito and Peter had tried to save it, she moaned. How heartbroken her brother had been when the bank foreclosed. It set Mary's teeth on edge.

She sensed it was doing worse to the man beside her. Jack shifted restlessly in his chair whenever Angie brought up the sensitive matter of the grocery store. After several verbal jabs, his mouth had tightened into a cold line. But to appease his mother, he suffered his aunt's implied blame in silence. Clearly, this wasn't easy for Jack, and Mary found herself admiring his restraint.

Yet she was more than ready to escape when Rose asked for her help getting the dessert. "My pigheaded sister-in-law's outdoing herself tonight," Rose declared as she handed Mary a bakery box full of cannoli. "Not only is she insulting Jack, but all this talk about the store is hurtful to Peter, too. He thinks he failed his father.''

Mary began placing the rich, cream-filled pastries on a crystal platter. ''Can't you say something to her?''

''I'd love to. But she's my Vito's only sister. I couldn't.'' Rose shook her head as she sliced a home-made coffee cake. ''Besides, she would only turn around anything we say and use it against my son. Then she would spread gossip about it all over the neighborhood. I don't want that for Jackie, now that he's come home.''

''I don't think he cares about the gossip. In fact, I'd bet he'd be more than happy to tell Angie off.''

''I know, I know. Jackie's always been able to take care of himself.'' Rose then surprised her with a fond look. ''I'm glad he has a friend in you, though.''

''We're not exactly friends.''

''That's what I thought,'' Rose claimed with such a triumphant smile that it was clear what she mistakenly presumed.

Before Mary could tell Rose she had it all wrong about her and Jack, the older woman had taken the hot coffeepot into the dining room. ''Wonderful, just wonderful,'' she mumbled under her breath. This was what she'd been afraid of—people thinking she and Jack were involved. A couple.

Yet, without warning, an image of the two of them walking back home, arm in arm, flashed through her mind. She closed her eyes, imagining how it would feel to have one of Jack's powerful arms wrapped around her shoulder, pulling her close against his side. She could practically feel his body's heat, as well as her reluctance to let go of it. At her apartment door, his dark, lustrous head would lower to hers for a kiss—not just a gentle good-night one, but a burning, soul-deep kiss that would tell her everything... about everything he wanted....

This vision lingered, the imagined sensations warming her all the way down to her toes. Mary reached out to the kitchen table to steady herself, and the cool Formica tabletop brought her back to reality in a hurry. Her eyes flew open. She was appalled at herself for fantasizing so vividly about a man she wanted to have as little to do with as possible. Wrong time, wrong place, wrong person! She was leaving Springfield in a matter of weeks. Nothing—and no one—was going to hold her back this time.

Deciding she would set the record straight as soon as Rose returned for the desserts, Mary kept her mind off fantasy kisses by refilling the sugar bowl and getting the milk out of the fridge for the cream pitcher. But it wasn't Rose who came for the cannoli. It was Angie.

For as long as she could remember, Jack's aunt had made Mary want to run the other way. Tonight was no exception. But there was no escaping. After picking up the platter of cannoli, Angie stared down at Mary with disapproving black eyes, and her tall, heavy body blocked the door to the dining room.

"Mary, I feel I must speak to you—for your own good," Angie said somberly. "You were just a child when Jack stole his father's savings and deserted this family. You can't know how selfish—"

"Angie, I don't think this is the time nor—"

"No—no—you must listen." The old woman stopped Mary with a brisk wave of her hand. "Don't you know my brother's health began running downhill the very day Jack ran away? He never recovered from the shock, so is it any wonder he lost the store?" Angie's voice quivered with twenty years' worth of fury. "Mark my words, that boy is the reason Vito died way before his time."

Mary stared back in disbelief—this woman was actually blaming Jack for his father's death. That did it, Mary decided, more livid than shocked. Jack may have done some pretty reprehensible things in the past, but this accusation was untrue, unfair and extremely cruel. Despite Rose's wishes, she could hold her tongue no longer.

"That store's days were numbered when the supermarket chain opened a big, shiny store at the shopping center. Everybody knew that," she said sharply, trying hard to keep her voice under control. "Vito knew it, too, but he was just too stubborn to make changes to counteract it."

"You know nothing about it!" shouted Angie.

"I heard plenty. My father and Vito used to argue about it all the time." At that point, Jack came in, followed by Rose and the rest of the family. Mary scarcely noticed; she was too wound up to stop, anyway. "All that had nothing to do with Jack. It just happened."

Angie's face reddened. "Don't defend that boy to me."

"I don't understand you, Angie. He's your brother's son, your flesh and blood, and he's finally come home. Can't you forgive the past and make the most of the time you can all have together?''

"Mary Piletti," Angie snapped as she dropped the platter of cannoli on the kitchen table, "did you lose all your good sense when Andy Mariano left you? Don't you know Jack'll break your heart just like he broke his family's?"

Mary was too astounded to answer, and suddenly Jack was standing between her and the old woman. "Leave Mary out of this, Angie," he said firmly, his eyes dark with anger. "If you have a problem—talk to me."

Angie didn't deign to answer him. "I'm leaving." She turned to Rose in a huff. "To think the day would come when I'd be insulted in my own brother's house."

"Now, Angie—" Rose began, but her sister-in-law would have none of it.

Instead Angie cast one last look at Mary. "Honestly, young lady, I thought you'd be smarter than to fall for the likes of Jack. Your parents must be crushed."

With that she swept out of the kitchen. A fretful Rose followed, beckoning to Peter to drive his aunt home. Gina hurried her children away, declaring it time for bed. Mary just stood there, mortified and relieved at the same time. And now, alone with Jack, she didn't know what to do.

He moved to her side, standing close, his hand on her shoulder. "There's only one thing I can say," he murmured. Despite the riotous sensations his touch on her bare skin was causing—or because of them—his low voice drew her gaze to his. When he smiled, his rich coffee eyes melted away her self-consciousness. "You, Mary Piletti, are quite a woman."

Mary had defended him. How long had it been since anyone had?

Walking Mary home from his mother's, Jack's mind was full of questions about her. No longer could he take the easy way out by brushing them aside. He wanted answers.

More than just her bold defense of him had sparked his need to know. The emotion blazing in her eyes when she told off Angie spoke volumes. Now he knew Mary couldn't be defined—or dismissed—as just a Peek Street girl. There was so much more inside of her, so much more to find out.

He glanced down at her as she strolled by his side. Glimmers of late-summer moonlight rippled through her dark hair. Mary was good-looking, intelligent and—as tonight had proven—she had a mind of her own. This was one woman who could take on the world. So why was she still here on Peek Street, unmarried and living within a stone's throw of her family?

Earlier today, in his apartment, she'd said something about plans getting waylaid by choice and circumstance. He hadn't pursued the matter further then because he didn't want to be drawn into her apparent restlessness. She might have told him things he didn't want to hear; things he didn't want to know.

Now he wanted to hear everything.

"Are you okay, Mary?" he asked as they waited for a car to pass before crossing the street.

"Oh, sure," she said, shrugging her shoulders. "Although I still feel terrible about causing trouble for your mother."

"You didn't. She said so herself." Jack fought the urge to caress her satiny shoulder tops. "Besides, Angie said some pretty embarrassing things. Not just to me, but to you."

Mary gazed straight ahead, saying nothing. But he knew she'd heard him.

"What's this about Andy Mariano?" he prodded. "I think I remember him. Neighborhood guy, right?"

"Was." Then she stopped and looked him right in the eye. "Andy and I used to be engaged."

"For how long?"

"Seven years."

He was surprised, and it must have shown, because Mary sighed and continued walking. "It's a long story, Jack."

"Tell me."

"Why?"

"Because I want to know why you're still here on Peek Street. Especially because I think you don't want to be."

"Ah, Jack, you don't want to get me started on that subject."

"Yes I do." They'd reached their building. The front stoop was deserted, the street was quiet. Jack sat down on the top step, patting the space beside him with one hand while reaching for Mary with the other. "Talk to me, Mary."

Reluctance was written all over her face, yet he gently tugged her arm until she joined him on the step. "Andy and I became formally engaged the day we graduated from high school," she finally began. "He gave me a ring and we sat down and planned out the next ten years of our lives."

"Ten years?"

She turned to him with a self-deprecating smile that struck him as rather alluring. "I used to be a great one for planning."

"I see." Actually, all he could see was her moist, full lips.

"Oh, yes," Mary continued, looking away nervously. "He was going to Princeton and then law school. I, being eminently practical, decided to save money by living at home while I earned my teaching degree. Then I'd teach, live at home and save more money for our marriage while Andy finished up law school. After all, he'd have a lot of student loans to pay off."

"I take it things didn't exactly work out that way."

"Actually they did—up until Andy's last semester of law school. That's when he fell passionately in love with a beautiful blond classmate."

"Passionately?"

"Andy's word."

The sympathy Jack felt for Mary was overshadowed by anger at Andy Mariano. What kind of jerk would add insult to injury by telling Mary of his passion for another woman? "Ah, you're better off without him."

Mary seemed startled by his reaction. "Probably," she agreed. "Though most people in this neighborhood still don't think so."

"I bet this was hot gossip for months."

"And months."

"Geez. Can't people around here mind their own business?" he said, shaking his head. "So why did you hang around, Mary? Why didn't you leave then?"

"Once I pulled myself together, I decided to use all that money I'd saved to go to graduate school in Washington," she explained. "Then, a few weeks before I was scheduled to move, Dad suffered a severe heart attack. It was touch and go for weeks. He had a bypass operation, but he was sick for a long time."

"So you stayed for your family."

"How could I leave? My mother was a wreck—helpless, really. Charlie had to take charge of the business, and his wife had just had their second baby. It was impossible."

"Your dad got better, though. Yet you're still here."

"It took quite a while for him—and Mama—to recover. By then I was well into a new teaching job and getting more involved in the consignment shop—which I eventually bought out. I never did get around to reapplying to grad school. So there was nothing to go to, no real reason to leave," she added, not sounding one bit sorry for herself. "But that's all changing now."

This bothered him. "Changing how?"

She gazed at him, her hazel eyes wavering with indecision. "Maybe it's best not to say yet," she said, slowly standing up. "One thing I've learned by now is not to count my chickens before they've hatched."

This vague reply irked him. As a man who liked to nail down an answer, he was tempted to push. After the scene in the kitchen with Aunt Angie, however, he'd learned something very basic about Mary Piletti: she didn't take well to being pushed. Not only did he respect that, he found it appealing as well. But damn, he wished he knew what she meant by *changing*.

"Mary—"

"It's late, Jack." She sounded wary.

Jack got to his feet, reaching out to her as she dug into her dress pocket for her keys. "Wait." His hand caught her elbow. "I haven't thanked you yet for defending my honor tonight—although I'm not quite sure you believe in it."

A bemused smile eased her tense expression. "You owe me one." She started to turn, but his hand remained firm on her arm. Her skin felt warm beneath his fingers. Now her smile turned cryptic. "Better be careful, Jack, or I may get it into my head to ask you a question or two."

The challenge in her husky voice flashed through his body like heat lightning, silent yet intense. He moved a step closer. "One thing I've learned is to be choosy about the questions I'll answer."

Mary's eyes glittered with amusement. "Ah, but you owe me—big." She was challenging him again. This time her voice radiated with such humorous warmth, he couldn't help but smile.

"You've got me there. I admit it, I *do* owe you big."

"So..."

"So ask your question."

"Just one?"

"Uh-huh. Because I've this gut feeling it's gonna be a doozy."

Laughing, she eased away from him and casually leaned back against the brick doorjamb. Jack couldn't keep his gaze from roaming the length of her body, from soft, round curves to beguiling, smooth angles.

Beneath the dim light hanging above the building's arched doorway, Mary's face glowed with amused speculation. The impact was bewitching. At that moment she could ask him any damn thing she wanted, and he knew he wouldn't—couldn't—refuse her.

Of course, Mary, with her schoolteacher's instinct, zeroed in on the question he always found hardest to answer. "Why did you run away all those years ago?" she asked.

With a sigh of resignation he turned away from her and sat back down on the top step. "I didn't think of it as running away. I still don't."

"No?" Mary had remained standing, so he couldn't see the expression on her face. But the skepticism in her single-word reply resounded loud and clear.

"Unlike you, Mary, I wasn't interested in planning out my entire life when I was eighteen years old," he said sharply, regretting his tone only for a moment. If Mary was going to ask tough questions, she'd better be prepared for the answers. He refused to offer a sugar-coated defense of himself. "But that's what my father wanted—demanded—from me."

"Maybe when you're eighteen it's easy to mistake a parent's hopes and wishes for demands."

"My father always made himself very clear," he explained. "He was adamant that I attend Springfield College or UMass, study business and eventually take over the store when he retired. That was the plan. No variation allowed."

"But, Jack," Mary protested, rejoining him on the steps again, "surely he—"

"Surely nothing, Mary. Look, when I graduated from high school I thought the world was mine. And

I wanted to see it—preferably from the seat of a bi-cycle." He glanced over at her. "I'd joined the local junior racing team, and I had developed into a strong racer. I wanted to turn pro."

Mary nodded. "Charlie told me."

"My dream was to race in the Tour de France," he added, remembering wistfully the pure joy that youthful dream had given him. "Of course, Dad dis-missed it as foolish nonsense. Not at all practical."

"A lot of fathers would, Jack."

"I know. But how many fathers would flat out re-fuse to give their kid a year—one year—to make a go of a dream. That's all I asked from my father, one lousy year."

"Vito wouldn't budge?"

"Not an inch." Jack shook his head. "So I swal-lowed it for a while, tried to be the dutiful son, like everyone expected. But my resentment grew until it finally dawned on me that a man doesn't wait around for permission to do what he wants. So I emptied out my college savings account—that's the money every-one says I stole from my father. It was a joint ac-count. I earned most of the money in it. And I left."

Mary looked him straight in the eye. "Just like that?"

"Pretty much," he admitted, returning her gaze. "I thought I knew the risk I was taking as far as my Dad was concerned. But it never struck home to my eigh-teen-year-old mind that the break would be perma-nent—that it'd be so hard to come back." He stared down at his hands. "As you and all of Springfield know, Dad and I never saw each other again."

"Didn't you ever try to come back?"

"Sure I did. When I got engaged to Sandra, I thought it'd be a chance to reconcile. I called Dad and said I wanted to bring her to meet the family."

"What did he say?"

"He asked who I was marrying and if I planned to come back to help with the store. When I told him we both intended to stay in Boston and build our careers, he cut me out again. Told me not to bother coming." He sighed, shaking his head. "As far as I was concerned, that was the end of it."

Admitting this out loud pained him more than he would've imagined. He rarely talked about what had happened all those years ago, and he wondered why he'd told Mary as much as he had. Now she sat silent beside him, her smooth shoulder barely grazing his arm. What was running through her mind? Renewed disapproval? After all, Mary Piletti was thirty years old and lived less than a mile from her parents and the house she grew up in. She must have a thing or two to say about a man who simply walked away from his family.

"Well, Mary?" he asked, feeling impatient.

She looked at him with unreadable eyes and shrugged her shoulders gently. "I know I've asked my allotted question, Jack. But I'd really like to know one more thing."

He nodded and waited for the dreaded, but inevitable follow-up question.

"Did you make it to the Tour de France?"

His mouth dropped. "What?"

"The Tour de France—your dream—did you race in it?"

That was not the question he'd expected. "Yes . . . yes, I did."

"Was it what you'd hoped it would be?"

Despite being caught off guard, he chuckled. "Aside from the fact that I finished way back in the pack, I'd say it was even better."

"I'm glad. That's how dreams should turn out."

From the golden warmth in her eyes, he could tell she meant it. "You're something else, Mary. Do you know that?"

"Me?" She shook her head.

"I thought you were going to ask if I had regrets about leaving the way I did."

Her eyes widened. "What would be the point of that? Besides, I don't think there's a person alive who doesn't have a regret or two."

Her matter-of-fact assurance was easing the pain of his disclosure considerably. Adding this to the way she'd defended him earlier made his heart feel lighter than it had since he'd returned to Springfield. Mary was not a royal pain, not by a long shot. She was pure treasure—a treasure almost buried by the lonely self-doubts about his return. Just being around her gave him a lift, and he was sorry he took so long to realize it. But he wasn't going to waste more time regretting that. Not now. Mary was here, he was back, time was on their side and the possibilities were, at the very least, intriguing.

"What are you smiling about now?" Mary asked, eyeing him with amusement.

Caught in the midst of thoughts he wasn't ready to share, Jack lightly tapped the tip of her nose with his finger. "You. I can't believe you got so much out of me tonight. Do you possess some sort of secret powers?" he teased. "Or perhaps you're some sort of sorceress from the old country."

"Hardly," she replied. Yet from the delicious grin on her face, he could tell that the notion pleased her. "You probably just needed to talk about why you left—now that you've come back."

Leaning back on his elbows, Jack gazed up at the hazy night sky. "'Now that I've come back.' Even now it seems strange. After everything that's happened, I'm back where I started. Maybe you and Charlie and Peter had the right idea all along. You all knew enough to stay put."

"I can't be included in that group, I'm afraid. Not anymore."

Puzzled, he turned to her. "What do you mean?"

There was no indecision surrounding her answer this time. "I'll probably be moving to Boston soon," she replied. "I'll finally be leaving Springfield."

Chapter Four

"Finally leaving? As in moving away?"

Mary nodded, her smoky eyes studying him with uncertainty. But that's about all Jack registered as he stared back, stunned. He felt as if he'd been whacked from behind with a two-by-four. So much for being prepared for tough answers!

"Why in hell would you do that?"

Mary stiffened, startled by his vehemence. "I beg your pardon?"

"You heard me."

"I don't have to explain myself to you."

She started to get up, but Jack grabbed her hands and held on, tight. "After I've just spilled my guts out to you about coming back, you say, 'That's nice. Oh, and by the way I'm leaving town'?" He shook his head. "I think I damn well deserve an explanation."

"Oh, I see what this is all about," Mary said, yanking her hands from his grasp. "It's about you. Now that the prodigal son has deigned to return home, everything on Peek Street should stop, and everyone's life should revolve around yours."

"You sound just like my brother, for Christ's sake," he snapped. "That's not how I feel and you know it."

"How can I know it? I barely know you, and you certainly don't know me."

Jack sighed. She was right about that. "Okay, Mary, tell me. Tell me what I need to know."

She turned her angry eyes away from him and stared straight ahead. At least she didn't bolt into the building. She began talking about prospective plans for used kids' clothing shops in the Boston area. From the enthusiastic lilt in her voice, Jack could tell she was serious about this possible partnership. And the ideas she detailed were sound, businesswise. Still, disappointment jabbed at him. Only minutes ago he had himself believing tonight was going to be the start of a beautiful relationship.

"Nothing's definite, of course," Mary continued, "which is why I was hesitant about mentioning it earlier—you know, counting my chickens and all that."

"I see."

"So? What do you think?"

"The idea sounds feasible, well thought out. You're obviously onto something. But," he added, unable to help himself, "allow me to play devil's advocate. If I may?"

She glared at him. "If you must."

He wasn't fazed. "Mary, here in Springfield you have an established business which, I gather, is doing well."

"Quite well."

"Yet you propose to start up another venture in Boston, a market unknown to you. A market that is, to say the least, different from Springfield."

"The Michaels are well acquainted with the Boston market."

"And that's good. But what about the economy? The reason I bought the shop I did is because it's established, a known entity here—I have a base to rebuild on. Starting a new business from scratch will be tricky."

"Naturally there are no guarantees, Jack. But the economy's been lousy. Don't you think our shops will fill a need—giving young families the chance to save money on clothes for their kids?"

Damn, he liked her. And it wasn't just the challenging flash of her gorgeous gold-green eyes that reminded him of the fact. Mary Piletti had backbone. Not only was she great at defending him to Aunt Angie, she stood up for herself, as well. It was a quality he admired, felt drawn to—maybe because he felt lacking in that particular strength when it came to dealing with the past, with Peek Street, with his family. By an unfortunate quirk of fate, however, she planned to leave just when he'd finally returned home. What a waste.

Then again he didn't have to be a total slave to fate. Jack eyed her solemnly. "Take it from me, Mary, life gets very cold out there."

"Life can get pretty harsh here on Peek Street, too," she said, meeting his gaze straight on. "We both know that, don't we?" It might be easier if she didn't have quite so much backbone, Jack thought dryly. Then again, he was stubborn. "But here you've always had your family to fall back on, no matter what. You've no idea what it's like to be on your own—all alone."

"And you have no idea what it's like to be a thirty-year-old woman who—for all intents and purposes—is still living under her father's roof," Mary countered, her voice rising with emotion. "I'm not naive enough to think it'll be a bed of roses out there. Of course I might fail. Of course I'll be lonely sometimes. But not to even try, not to ever know if I could do it would be much, much worse. You, of all people, should understand."

Jack didn't respond right away; the answer he had intended to give, he couldn't. Because he did understand. Her impassioned argument, the earnest expression on her face—he understood those all too well. Yet he'd been so absorbed by his attraction to her that he'd underestimated the intensity of her dream. Well, didn't everyone say he was selfish?

"Jack, try to see where I'm coming from," Mary said, apparently taking his silence for disapproval. "The restlessness you felt when you were eighteen, that desire to get out there and spread your wings, I'm just experiencing now." She shrugged her shoulders. "Guess I'm a late bloomer."

He shook his head. "Everyone's on their own timetable. There's no shame in that."

"My own timetable," she echoed. "I like that. Makes me feel less—less slow."

"You should go for it, Mary," he offered gently. "Really, I hope it works out." He meant it, but he didn't like it.

"Thanks. I need all the good thoughts I can get." She gave his arm a slight squeeze, and this touch pulled his gaze to hers like a magnet. Her wide hazel eyes and distinctive smile made his pulse hum—again. This time he fought the sensation.

He had to put some distance between them. Now. He straightened, removing his arm from her hazardous clasp to check his watch. "Look how late it's gotten."

"Heavens. We've been yakking up a storm." She stood up to go inside.

Jack remained seated on the top step. "I think I'll stay out here a few more minutes."

She hovered above him, confusion crossing her face. After an awkward pause, she finally said goodnight. As she whisked through the door, traces of her perfume swirled around him, kindling a surge of regret. But regret was something he'd sworn to discard from his life. Perhaps he should've paid better attention to his initial instinct regarding Mary Piletti—the one that warned hands-off.

After all, he'd come home to straighten out his life, not complicate it.

Mary slid the dead bolt into place and collapsed against her apartment door, annoyed and relieved. Annoyed because of the way Jack had summarily dismissed her just now. Relieved because here, alone, she was safe from the gamut of emotions their conversations provoked. She had to be on her toes with every word she said to him, but the exercise made her feel quick, vibrant. Being with Jack tonight had been exhilarating. On the other hand, being with Jack could prove dangerously addictive. She couldn't afford that. Not now.

Still, it was all she could do to keep herself from unlocking the door and rushing back for another dose of his sharp wit and another glimmer of his sexy, dark eyes. To make sure she didn't, she slipped off her dress and went to the closet. She pulled on a jade green nightshirt, its light cotton fabric soothing and cool against her flushed skin. Despite the late hour, it still had felt hot outside. She flicked on the air conditioner in the bedroom.

Mary plopped on top of her bed, letting the cold blast from the window unit wash over her. Unable to shake Jack from her mind, she wondered why. Had this one night changed the dynamics that much? Maybe so. The bitter stories of blind selfishness that Vito and Angie Candelaria had perpetuated over the years had left her unprepared for the reality of the man. Tonight, after hearing his side of the story, she felt a kinship with him. That Jack had gone off to follow his dream despite the risks intrigued her enormously. This, above all else, had struck a chord with her.

The red blinking light on the answering machine caught her eye. Reaching over to the nightstand, she pressed the Play button and soon heard Lorna Michael identifying herself. "... Since we talked to you this morning, Terry and I've been working up a business plan for the shops, and we want your ideas and comments. Hope to have it to you by the end of the week.''

The message snapped her back to reality. She could not permit any distractions from her plans. She couldn't risk ending up empty-handed again. Although she reacted strongly to Jack on many levels, and in ways she hadn't felt since Andy, she mustn't forget they were traveling in two different directions. He'd come home to roost; she was ready to fly away.

The next morning Mary drove to her parents' house after ten-thirty Mass, as she usually did. Except for her mother, busy preparing Sunday dinner in the kitchen, the place was uncharacteristically quiet. ''Where is everybody?'' she asked, giving her mother a kiss on the cheek. ''Charlie and his brood weren't at church.''

''They went earlier. Little Lisa's swim team's having their big picnic today at Forest Park,'' Josephine Piletti explained, as she chopped Swiss chard, fresh from the backyard garden. ''So it's just the three of us for dinner today.''

''And where's Dad?'' Mary opened the oven door a crack to find a glazed ham baking.

''Showing a house to one of Charlie's clients. He'll be back soon.'' Glancing over her shoulder at Mary, Josephine added, ''Good thing I had that ham in the refrigerator. I didn't think you'd want manicotti two meals in a row.''

Closing the oven door, Mary straightened. ''So, you've talked to Rose Candelaria already today?''

''No—Angie. After Mass this morning.''

Mary sighed. She should've known.

"Must've been quite the family gathering," Josephine continued, "what with Jack there and all."

Considering Angie's frame of mind last night, and knowing her own mother all too well, Mary knew what was coming. She might as well meet it head-on. "Mother, there's nothing going on between me and Jack Candelaria."

"That's not what Angie says."

"Oh, and does Angie also say I'm on the road to ruin?"

"More or less." Josephine poured olive oil into a heavy iron frying pan and lighted the gas burner beneath it.

"Well, you don't have to worry. Jack and I are not an item."

"I wouldn't be worried if you were."

"You mean to say it wouldn't bother you if your one-and-only daughter was mixed up with the renowned black sheep of Peek Street?"

Her mother tossed the Swiss chard in the heated pan. "I, for one, never believed Jack was all bad. Sure, he's made mistakes—bad ones. But he's Rose's son. He's got to have some of her goodness in him. You could do worse."

"I could?" she said, surprised. But on second thought she realized her parents had rarely spoken of Jack Candelaria through the years. Jack had detractors all over Peek Street, but not in the Piletti household. Mary was sure her parents kept their counsel out of respect for Rose. "A lot of people wouldn't share that opinion with you, Mom."

"Mary Regina Piletti—when has that ever mattered to me? I know what I know and—"

"And I think what I think," Mary finished, giving her mother's round shoulders an affectionate squeeze. In spite of a strict, old-world upbringing, Josephine was an outspoken, independent thinker. Mary had always been proud of that.

Josephine stirred the chard as the delicious smell of greens simmering in olive oil and a bit of garlic filled the kitchen. "Anyway, Jack can't possibly be in the picture when you're bound and determined to start that new business in Boston. Right?"

Mary didn't like the way that sounded. "I thought you were glad for me."

"Of course I'm glad. Haven't I always encouraged you to do what you need to do?"

"Yes," Mary admitted, reaching toward the glass-doored cabinet that held the Sunday china and glassware, "you're always supportive."

"And your father, too," Josephine added. "No matter how he really feels..."

"Wait a minute. Dad sat at that table the other night and agreed this was a great opportunity for me."

"He knows it is, he knows." Turning from the stove, Josephine patted her chest. "But in his heart, he'd rather keep you and Charlie close by forever. He wishes you had a husband to take care of you...children. He'd never say that, though. And he shouldn't. You're both grown-up adults who have to live your own lives."

Mary knew her mother meant what she'd said. Her parents never intentionally held her back. They were the best, she thought warmly, really the best. As she took three wineglasses off the shelf, a car door slammed outside.

"There's your father now." Josephine turned off the stove and wiped her hands on her apron. "You go set the table. And not a word about what I just told you. It would embarrass him."

Mary had just about finished setting the dining room table when Mario Piletti came in carrying a carafe of white wine. With the sleeves of his good white shirt rolled up and with his Sunday tie pulled loose, he looked his usual rumpled self. "Your mother says the ham'll be ready in five minutes," he announced.

She greeted him with a smile. "How'd your appointment go?"

"Ah, a waste of time. I showed this young couple the Feeney place over on Barnes, and they had absolutely no interest in it."

"Really? That's such a great house." Although it was technically outside their neighborhood, Mary remembered trick-or-treating there back when her dad was friendly with old Mr. Feeney. He had built the big yellow house with black shutters during the twenties.

"I don't know where Charlie finds his clients." Shaking his head, Mario sat down at the head of the table. "These people said it was too old and too big. Okay, I accept that. But then they tell me they don't want children. Married three months and they've already decided such a thing. Can you believe it?"

"I wouldn't know about that, Dad. But I can imagine some people might consider the Feeney place a bit of a white elephant. You have to love that kind of house to see the possibilities, not to mention having the money and desire to fix it up," she said. "I bet it needs a lot of updating."

Mario shrugged. "Maybe it's just as well they weren't interested. Sally Feeney's been real skittish about it. Some days she's clamoring for a sale, other days she wants to hang on to it."

"She's lived there all her life. It must be hard to let go."

"Shame she never married, then she could've passed it on to her kids. I tell you, Mary, it's sad to have to deal with these things when you're all alone."

Mary picked up the carafe of wine. No way was she going to touch that last remark.

Mario leaned back, watching as she poured wine into each glass. "So, I heard you had supper at the Candelarias' last night. With Jack."

"Don't tell me Angie talked to you, too."

"No—Rose." He sampled the wine in his glass before adding, "She also said you gave Angie a piece of your mind. Never seen anyone do that before."

"I know I shouldn't have spoken to her like that. But honestly, Dad, the way she was treating Jack was abominable," she insisted. "And as far as I can tell, what Jack did twenty years ago wasn't so horrible."

Her father's bushy white brows lifted in surprise. "You know what Jack did?"

"He told me all about it last night. And I believe him," she hastened to add.

"Do you?"

The way her father looked at her made her feel defensive. "Any reason why I shouldn't?"

"I suppose he put the blame on Vito."

"He didn't come out and say that, but it's clear from the facts that his father created an impossible situation."

"Facts are funny things," Mario said, drumming his fingers on the table. "Twenty years ago, when I was raising you and your brother, and when Vito was my closest friend, the facts looked very different. To me, Jack took off for his own selfish reasons and broke his mother's heart. As a father, I didn't care about anything else."

Now Mary was surprised. "But in all these years, you never said a word against Jack."

"Out of respect for Rose. She was devastated by this, and there was too much talk flying around as it was," Mario explained. "Besides, in time I came to feel differently. The facts, as you call them, weren't quite so clear."

"What happened?"

"Vito became very bitter, self-destructive. He lost the store through his own pigheadedness, and he made Peter's life hell," he said, shaking his head with regret. "But even worse, Jack wanted to come home a few times, and Vito turned him away. Disowned him, actually."

"How could he do a thing like that?"

"I asked myself the same thing. How can a father wash his hands of his own flesh and blood?" Mario shrugged. "Who can say why Vito did it? He wasn't a bad man, believe me. But I think maybe his soul got lost along the way."

"Is this why you offered to help Jack find a place to live?"

"Sure. It's good he's come back. Good for Rose, especially. And around here, he's gonna need all the friends he can get." He shot her a sly smile. "Like you telling Angie off for him."

She shook her head at the reminder. "She really did deserve it, Dad."

He chuckled with delight. "Wish I'd been there."

Riding into the parking lot, Jack spotted Mary getting out of her car. As she stepped onto the pavement, her body and legs flowed in a graceful, even line. It was this fluid, unselfconscious movement that kept her from appearing a tad too schoolmarmish in the crisp navy blue suit she wore. But thanks to that long, smooth curve of glossy dark hair, schoolmarmish was a tag a man would never pin on Mary Piletti. Not this man, anyway.

Damn, why did he have to run into her again? After she left last night, he'd convinced himself that a moderate degree of distancing would quickly dispel the fascination she held for him. At the time it'd seemed the best action to take and easy enough to accomplish. Although he and Mary lived in the same building, they'd rarely bumped into each other. Except for now. But she hadn't noticed him yet, so he could take another swing around the block and avoid her altogether.

"Candelaria," he muttered under his breath, "you're too old for that game."

He pulled up beside her as she locked the car door. "Hey, Mary. You're all dressed up."

"For church this morning."

It was now five in the afternoon. He wondered where she'd spent the rest of her day and with whom. "It's been a great day, hasn't it? Much cooler," he said, unfastening his cycling helmet.

She smiled. "You look like you've been taking advantage of it."

"I'm testing out a new model—the latest in twelve-speed technology." He looped the helmet's strap on the hook of the down-turned handlebars. "And I like to get out to ride whenever I can. The shop keeps me awfully busy, though."

"Having second thoughts? About your new business, I mean?"

"It's been hectic getting started, but I'm loving it. Trust me, selling bicycles is a vast improvement over selling stock. I have my sanity back."

Mary rested lazily against her car, listening, and Jack realized how glad he was that he hadn't decided to avoid her. He found himself telling her about the help he'd hired: Leo, the aging hippie who'd begun repairing bikes for the previous owner in 1969; Fred, a retiree who'd become an avid bicyclist at sixty-five; and Randy, a college kid who would help out part-time.

So much for distancing.

He had no idea how long they stood there talking. He always lost track of time when he was with Mary. And what was so bad about that? If he was having second thoughts about anything, it was about the conclusion he'd come to last night. Sure, she'd be leaving town in the not-so-distant future, but was that enough reason to deny himself her company, her friendship? Come what may, he could handle it.

He leaned on the handlebars. "Why don't you come bicycling with me next Sunday? I'd rather have company than go alone."

"Are you kidding? I haven't ridden a bike in years. You need someone who can keep up with you."

"You're gonna have to take pity on me, Mary. You're just about the only friend I have around here. Look, you've shown more interest in my shop than my own brother has. He won't even give me the time of day," he said, though he knew playing on her sympathy wasn't exactly fair. "It would mean a lot to me if you came, and I know some gorgeous routes out toward the Berkshires that aren't difficult at all."

"Jack, I don't think we should go out together."

He wasn't foolish enough to ask why; he knew she could come up with several reasons. All of them valid. Yet one unimpeachable argument came to mind. "It's too late to worry that people might think we're involved. Aunt Angie will probably tell the entire neighborhood that we are."

"She already has. She got hold of my mother this morning at seven-thirty Mass." Mary grimaced and then laughed at the irony of it.

"So, we might as well get some mileage out of it."

She hesitated, clearly torn about what to do. He took heart that she probably wanted to go with him, yet he was a little annoyed that she was fighting it. She might like him in spite of herself, but hell, she still didn't trust him.

Maybe he should let her off the hook. That would be the gallant, unselfish thing to do, especially when he didn't exactly know what he wanted from her. Yet as he looked at her, tawny skin glowing in the late-afternoon light and rose-tinted mouth almost irresistible, Jack felt the possibilities too enticing to sacrifice.

"Mary?"

She met his gaze. "Jack, I want to," she admitted, then added hastily, "but I can't. I don't even own a bike."

Feeble, Mary, very feeble, he thought, feeling an amused stab of affection for her stubbornness.

"You've forgotten something, Mary."

"What?"

"I own a store full of them."

Chapter Five

She never should've accepted.

Mary told herself this for the umpteenth time that week as she fetched a tube of sunscreen from the medicine cabinet. She'd almost canceled the bike ride several times. Almost. But she never could bring herself to go up to Jack's apartment and tell him she wasn't going. Phoning proved no easier. Even the Michael sisters' business plan, which she received Friday afternoon, didn't provide the push she needed to call the whole thing off.

It wasn't lack of nerve, however, that stopped her from doing what she was convinced was the smart thing. No, it was lack of good, sound reason. She didn't seem to have any when it came to Jack Candelaria. All he had to do was pedal into the parking lot and her resolve to stay away from him dissolved. She knew he was angling for sympathy by saying she was his only friend here. She knew and it worked anyway—with a little help from soul-stirring eyes and a persuasiveness that could charm snakes.

Now she was slathering white sun goop on her arms and legs while trying to decide what to wear for an afternoon of cycling. Deep down, though, Mary had to admit she was excited about spending the day with Jack, ill-advised as it might be. She chuckled ruefully. She might be protecting her skin from sunburn, but she was also setting her body up for some sore muscles on Monday. And possibly worse as far as she and Jack were concerned.

She met him in front of Jack's Cycles promptly at ten. Her heart did tiny flips at the sight of him, cool and handsome in a bright white cotton T-shirt and drawstring shorts. His muscular thighs and calves, strong, tight and tanned, were evidence of his athleticism. And they were just plain nice to look at, as well. Not wanting to ogle, Mary glanced down at her own outfit, an oversize pink T-shirt, billowing coolly around her, and mint green Lycra bicycle shorts, which she wore only to exercise class. "I hope this is appropriate."

"Just right." Smiling, Jack unlocked the shop's door and held it open for her. "Come on in."

When he switched on the lights, Mary's eyes combed over racks of bicycles in every style, shape, size and color. The array of sleek designs was mind-boggling for someone who'd owned only two bikes in her life, a squat two-wheeler with foot brakes and a second-hand, three-speed English model. Accessories lined the walls in neat display—helmets, lights, air pumps, saddlebags, car racks, child carriers. Jack pointed out the office and repair room in the rear of the shop, and then he showed her the corner he planned to devote to children's bikes.

"It'll take some time to get it exactly the way I want, but we're evolving." He turned to her, arms spread wide. "What do you think?"

His pride was obvious and well warranted. She found his concern about her opinion endearing, if out of character. It was a shame his family had shown no interest in the shop. "I like it a lot," she told him. "Looks like you're on the right track."

He led her over to an open space and began eyeing her from head to toe. As his gaze meandered back up over her hips and breasts, her pulse leapt. Disconcerted, she snapped, "Is something wrong?"

"Not a thing," he drawled. Yet his gaze lingered, embracing her with what felt like a magic spell—a spell that fueled the soaring beat of her heart with the warmth from his brown eyes. Finally Jack broke this hold by turning to the rack of bikes behind him. "You're about five-five, right?"

"Five-six." She wondered if she sounded as off kilter as she felt.

"Close enough." He pulled a blue medium-size multispeed from the rack and wheeled it beside her. Holding the handlebars steady, Jack asked her to straddle the frame. When she did, both feet were planted flat on the floor. "Good," he murmured, moving to her side. "Now try the saddle."

As she lifted her buttocks onto the leather seat, Jack placed a guiding hand on the small of her back. It was a simple touch, certainly not intimate, yet her mind zoomed in on the pleasurable pressure. She scarcely heard him complain that her feet were still flat on the floor.

Crouching lower, his hand slid from her back and he rotated the pedals until one was all the way down. "Rest the ball of your foot on this one." Then his warm hand skimmed along her thigh to her knee, making her limbs feel as weak as a newborn foal's. As if he sensed this, he looked up, half-apologetically. "Just checking your form. See, your knee's too bent." His hand trailed down her bare calf to her ankle. "And your heel should be higher than your toes. Seems your legs are on the long side."

"Sorry," she mumbled, trying to regain control over her voice as well as her tingling nerve endings.

"You shouldn't be," he rasped, looking up. His palm remained curved on her skin as they exchanged glances, and Mary realized he, too, felt the tension sparking the air. It wasn't just her; it wasn't one-sided. Yet her head spun like a confused top because she felt thrilled and panicky at the same time.

"I'll raise the saddle a bit after we check the handlebars." To her relief, Jack stood up. Still beside her, he balanced the bike by gripping the dropped bars and the back edge of the seat. "Now sit in riding position, both feet on the pedals."

Mary couldn't suppress a wince of doubt.

"Don't worry, I won't let you fall."

His hold was so firm that the bike didn't even teeter when she positioned her feet on the pedals.

"Okay?"

"Okay." At least she guessed she was. It was hard to think straight when he stood so close she could

smell the fresh scent of his soap. The feeling of being
suspended on air muddled her thinking further, as she
marveled at balancing with both feet off the ground.
In her utterly distracted frame of mind, this was solid
proof of Jack's physical strength, something she had
speculated about more than once.

"Okay, now dangle your left arm by your side," he
told her, "and then rotate it forward in a large arc. But
don't stretch."

Her hand landed smack dab on the handlebars.

"Perfect." He smiled and his hand covered hers for
a moment. "Only the seat needs adjustment. I'll do it
out back. Won't take a second."

The gleam in his eyes belied the nonchalance in his
voice. Not sure she could sound as detached, Mary
said nothing as she carefully dismounted. But as she
watched him take the bike away, she realized she was
in trouble. This tug-of-war attraction was no longer a
game played in the safety of her thoughts—where she
had total control. With a touch and a look that spoke
volumes, Jack had become an active player, and an
undeniable mutual awareness changed all the rules.

Oh yes, she was in trouble here. Big trouble.

Jack glanced over his shoulder at the blue-helmeted
cyclist bobbing behind him and smiled. Although
she'd made a fuss about being out of shape, Mary was
keeping up. She seemed to be enjoying herself. And
why not? It was a glorious day, neither too hot nor
humid. For her sake he'd chosen one of the easier
routes he knew of among the low mountains and ver-
dant countryside of the Berkshires. Maintaining a
natural, easy cruising speed, they rode along gently

rolling hills and back roads, past idyllic homesteads and pristine pastures. Fresh, clean air, beautiful scenery, charming company—it didn't get much better than this.

Slowing down a bit, he gestured to Mary to pull up alongside him. "How's it going?"

"Are my legs still moving?" she cracked with some huffing and puffing. "How far have we ridden?"

"Only ten miles or so from where we left the car."

"Only?"

"Well, we've taken three or four more rest stops than I normally do." He shot her a teasing grin.

"You're too kind." But she smiled back.

"Hungry?"

"Ravenous. Why don't we stop right along here?"

"Uh-uh. I've chosen a great spot with a knockout view."

She groaned as they maneuvered a wide bend in the deserted road. "How much farther is this great spot?"

Reaching the end of the curve, he pointed ahead. "At the crest of that hill."

"You've got to be kidding."

"The view is worth it. Trust me."

"Hah! Trusting you has taken me only ten long, bone-numbing, breath-robbing miles."

He really liked her spirit. "I knew you were having fun."

Mary laughed. "Actually, I am."

They continued in companionable silence until they approached the base of the hill. Mary took one look and let out a low wail of disbelief. "Whoa. That's much steeper than it first looked."

"Yeah, I know," he agreed. It was one of the steepest inclines around here. Still, the rest of the route was easy enough that he'd figured the hill wouldn't be too much of a problem for her.

"Maybe we could just walk it," she suggested, "and save our energy for lunch."

"Walk it? Ah, Mary, it's not that bad. You can do it."

Slowing a bit, she glanced over at him. "Maybe I can. But do I want to? It's really not an ego thing for me, and I'd like to be able to walk tomorrow."

"Just drop into a low gear and take it slow and easy. You'll be fine," he assured. "Besides, Mary, you're not the type to wimp out. You've broken up a fight between my brother and me—twice!"

"You're just trying to egg me on, aren't you?" she accused sharply. "Next thing I know, you'll want to race me up that thing."

Stifling a laugh, he shook his head. "Nah, that wouldn't be fair."

She muttered something unintelligible.

"Pardon? I couldn't make that out, Mary."

"Look, Jack, I'm going to do it—to see if I can. But if I feel like my legs are about to fall off, I'm stopping and walking. And," she added with a stern school-teacher glare, "if I do walk, I expect no comments from you."

"Yes, ma'am." He gave her a mock salute. "I'll just wait for you at the top with lips zipped."

Climbing the hill, he kept his pace moderate, and Mary kept up with him for a while. But when she fell behind, he said nothing, and he thought better of glancing back over his shoulder. She'd hate that. So he maintained speed, not too slow as to insult her, nor too fast to discourage her. Reaching the crest, he pulled over to the wide, grassy shoulder and finally allowed himself a look at Mary's progress.

She was only about midway, but she was still pedaling, God love her. Tossing his safety helmet to the ground, he swept his soaked forehead with the back of his arm. To cool his muscles and even his breathing, he walked in a big circle, keeping an eye on Mary all the while. He took a swig from his water bottle. Mary plodded on. "That's right, keep it steady," he urged, murmuring to himself. "Save it for the last push."

Jack grinned. Although Mary was wobbling a bit from fatigue as she broached the final short stretch to the peak, he knew she'd make it. The woman was something else. Be it taking on an intimidating hill or venturing into the dining room of a warring family, Mary Piletti did not shrink from challenge. He knew that for certain.

He applauded loudly as Mary coasted past. She looped back quickly and joined him at the side of the road. Breathing hard, she jumped off the bike and collapsed on the grass. "I don't believe I did that," she gasped. "Water...please..."

Jack unhooked the water bottle from her bicycle's down tube. Sitting up, Mary pulled off her helmet and grabbed the bottle at the same time. "Thanks," she said, exhaling after one last gulp. She fell back again, her arms flung out wide. "I guess I'll survive, but I'm never moving from this spot."

"Stop and walk, my foot," he sniffed, sitting down by her side. "Who'd you think you were fooling?"

Her eyes closed. "Apparently not you. Believe me, though, I'm gonna pay for this tomorrow."

"Nah, you're in great shape." Which was the God-honest truth, he realized, as his gaze roamed over her lush body. Every inch of her exposed skin glistened with perspiration. This sheen, highlighting the delicate arc of her throat and the feminine curves of her limbs, struck him as tantalizingly erotic. She was still panting a little, too. The quickened rise and fall of her soft breasts taunted him. His fingers ached to touch them, cup their softness—her softness, and it was all he could do to restrain the urge. But restraint held no sway over the ache of desire vibrating through him.

He focused on her face, moist and smooth, looking finely sculpted and very womanly with her ebony hair pulled back into one sleek braid. He felt his body tense, his breathing grow ragged. How he'd love to stretch out alongside her and fold her body into his. It would feel so good, so soothing, yet so hot. Lord, he wanted nothing more than to make love to her right here and now.

Of course, if he actually tried, she'd never let him near her again. Ever.

Dragging himself back to reality, Jack swallowed hard and forced himself to stand. "I thought you were hungry. Our picnic spot is just a few yards away."

Her eyes popped open. "I think I lost my appetite about halfway up here. Besides, didn't you hear me? I'm not moving."

"You'll feel better once you get a load of this view. It'll make you forget everything."

"Even my aches and pains?" she demanded. But her frown of resistance gradually curved into a receptive grin, and she held out her hand. "Okay, take me away. I want the last fifteen minutes wiped from my memory forever."

"Not me. I'll always remember." Slinging the saddlebag over his shoulder, he pulled Mary to her feet.

They walked their bikes on the grass for several yards until they reached a huge gray boulder. They rested the bikes against it. "Now close your eyes," he ordered.

Without so much as a squawk of protest, she let him lead her around the boulder. He stopped at the spot he considered the optimum vantage point. "Okay, take a look."

She looked straight ahead and her face lit up with delight. "Oh, Jack..."

He followed her gaze as it spanned across the sweeping view of open fields and woodlands, dotted here and there with ponds and lakes, which seemed to shimmer in the sunlight. All sizes of hills rolled through the panorama below, some covered by a luxuriant green blanket of late-summer foliage. An early sprinkling of pale yellow kissed the occasional tree, a promise of the blazing glory soon to come.

Finally Mary turned to him, her eyes full of the same wonder he'd always experienced here. "This was definitely worth it. Thank you for bringing me up here."

Then and there, Jack decided he'd bring her back in the fall. "Local cyclists call this Splendor Bluff."

"I can see why." Mary drank in the vista for untold minutes.

"You can feast your eyes all you want while we eat," he assured her.

Emptying the saddlebag, he handed Mary a light plastic tarp to unfold on the grass. Then he brought out sandwiches, fruit and individual bottles of spring water and placed them on the tarp. "There you go, hotshot. Dig in."

"At last," she declared, unwrapping a sandwich quickly. She held up the sizable pita pocket stuffed with seasoned chicken chunks, thin tomato slices and shredded lettuce. "This is gorgeous. Don't tell me you made these?"

"I got them at the deli a few doors down from the shop." Before he had finished answering, she was hungrily tearing into the sandwich. He smiled wryly. "Gee, Mary, will one be enough for you? Maybe I should give you half of mine, too."

She made a face, but kept munching contentedly.

After consuming her sandwich—but not his—a handful of white grapes and a large Granny Smith apple, Mary drained the last of her spring water. She lay on her back and sighed. "That was wonderful, Jack. Now all I need is a nap."

"While I think your appetite is admirable," he said, stowing the carefully wrapped trash in the saddlebag, "a nap is not the way to top it off. Not if you want to get back on that bike."

She grimaced. "Did I make a pig of myself?"

"Hardly." He stretched out on his side, resting his head on his bent arm. "Besides, you did some strenuous exercising today—you needed to refuel."

"Refuel—I like that. Sounds much more dignified than pigging out."

He laughed, shaking his head. "Mary, I am glad you came today. This definitely beats riding alone."

"You mean it's more amusing?"

"That, too." He gazed at her profile, finding the combination of strong features and creamy skin provocative. He would've loved to trail his fingertip along her smooth cheek, but thought better of it. He'd hate to wreck this convivial mood by scaring her, or worse, dislodging the small modicum of trust he was establishing with her.

"Will you come riding with me again?" he asked instead.

Her eyes narrowed. "Not without advance notice of killer hills."

"You've got it." He made a great show of crossing his heart. "I promise."

"Well, we'll see."

"You know, I half expected you to come up with a reason to back out of this."

Chuckling, Mary turned onto her side to face him. "I came up with several, actually. But after I told my folks I wouldn't be at dinner today, I felt committed."

"Did you tell them you were going out with me?"

She paused a second, a furtive look in her eye. "Well, not exactly. I said I was visiting an old friend."

"Mary Piletti, lying to your parents at your age? I can hardly believe it."

"Go ahead, tease. I just thought it wiser not to feed the speculation about you and me."

"Guess I should be grateful that you came at all," he said, shrugging. "So why did you decide to come? Did you feel sorry for me?"

"There was that aspect," she agreed, eyes twinkling. "But the ride sounded fun, too. And, despite my griping, I'm enjoying myself. You're not so bad to be around.''

"Do me a favor and tell that to my legions of fans in the neighborhood.''

"I plan to.'' She sounded serious.

"Thanks.'' Holding her gaze, he lowered his hand to her forearm, his fingers skimming across her soft skin. "I need a friend around here, especially someone open-minded like you.''

"Jack, people will come around in time. Even your brother.''

"I'm not sure about him. You know, when I decided to come back, it never occurred to me that Peter would be this hostile and angry.'' He shook his head. "So much for foresight.''

"Jack, why did you decide to come back now—after twenty years?''

"Seemed as good a time as any.''

"Because your wife had died?''

"That had a lot to do with it.''

"It must've been devastating. You must've felt so alone.''

Mary was sensitive and compassionate—sweet, really. But she didn't have a clue—not about the whys and wherefores of his life before he came back. And he wasn't about to tell her about Sandra and their nine-year marriage. He didn't know if he wanted to; he wasn't sure he could. The wound was still raw.

But Mary cared, that's what mattered. He had so little of that in his life lately. He leaned over to plant a kiss on her cheek. "You're the only one in all of Springfield who's even asked about my wife.''

Aside from the initial flicker of surprise, her expression was unreadable. Still, she didn't press for explanations, for which he was thankful. A day such as this, full of fun and life, was too precious to be shadowed by the past.

"Time to get a move on," he said, sitting up. "The car's a few more miles away."

"But it feels like we just got here. Can't we stay just a little longer?"

"Take heart, Mare. If you thought this view was worth the climb up that hill, the real payoff is reeling back down it. Get ready to be exhilarated out of your mind."

Jack decided to drop Mary off at the apartment building before returning the bikes to the shop. They had stopped for a hearty dinner at an old diner Mary knew off the turnpike, and now it was pretty late. Still, he was sorry to see their day end.

He walked her to the front door. "With a little time and practice, you're going to make a fantastic cyclist, Mary."

"As far as I'm concerned, the jury's out until my muscles have a chance for rebuttal. So don't get your hopes up, Candelaria."

Mary gave as good as she got, and he loved it. "Sorry, hon, but I'm a stubborn fool when it comes to hope," he replied, grinning. "Wouldn't have come back to Springfield if I wasn't."

Tilting her head slightly, Mary studied his face for a moment. "You should smile more often."

"I don't smile?"

"Not like that," she said. "You crack a sly, know-it-all kind of grin now and then, but—"

"Know-it-all?" he repeated, feigning offense while contemplating how attracted to her he was right now. "Guess that puts me in my place."

"No—Jack—I didn't mean it like that." She pressed her palms against his chest in protest.

This touch propelled him into action. "Come here, Mary." He slid his arms around her waist, pulling her taut against him.

Her eyes widened as their bodies made contact. Hands splayed across his white shirt. She stared up at him, uttering not a sound.

His gaze lingered on her slightly parted lips—the lips he'd been wanting for days. "You know, I think you like me in spite of yourself."

Her quick glimmer of a smile told him he was right. The way her body softened in his arms told him even more: her resistance was melting—in spite of herself.

Jack focused on her face, strong yet womanly. Lovely. Damn, it was tempting. To lower his head to hers, to finally taste her soft, full mouth, to kiss it deep and long and well. His blood hummed, the pressure low in his body intensifying.

His embrace quickened with emerging desire, holding Mary closer, tighter. He searched her eyes, hoping to find the same heat that was simmering within him. "Mary," he murmured in an urgent whisper, bringing his lips closer to hers.

She stiffened in his arms, her gaze suddenly a closed book. Then she pulled away, dazed. "This isn't a—"

Vexed by this sudden resistance, he cut her off by reaching for her hand and holding on tight. "I want to see you again."

She didn't answer.

"I won't pretend otherwise, and neither should you."

"Okay, okay, I may want to see you again," she conceded. "It's just not a good idea."

"We're not talking ideas here, Mary Piletti," he declared, barely keeping his frustration at bay. He wished she'd quit trying to be rational when all he wanted was to kiss her until her knees trembled.

Mary closed her eyes with a sigh. "I'll be moving away soon—you know that. I don't want to start anything."

Peering down into her eyes, he squeezed her hand. "It's already started."

She gave no answer. She just pulled her hand away.

He didn't care. "Come to my place for dinner on Wednesday night."

Her mouth dropped. Clearly she hadn't expected him to persist. "Sorry, but this is an extremely busy time for me. Not only do I have a business plan to review, it's also the busiest season at my store. I've got new inventory to tag and move in, and old stuff to move—"

"Let me put it this way, Mary," he interjected quickly, realizing he'd better put a hold to this litany of excuses before his invitation ended up dead in the water. "My shop closes early on Wednesdays, so I'm going to be home cooking anyway. If you find yourself with a spare hour or two that evening, come on up. I'll set a place for you . . . just in case."

Jack returned to his car, leaving her at a total loss for words. Mary fumed. He was, by far, the most infuriating man she'd ever met. She'd had every reason to reject his dinner invitation—especially when he looked at her as if she would be the main course. But no, it wasn't in his Candelaria nature to accept a simple refusal. Jack had to turn it into an open invitation and lob it into her court, drop it in her lap.

The man was as impossible as his family!

"And impossible to get rid of," she told herself as she fumbled with the front door keys. Yet a nagging voice within her insisted it was nobody's fault but her own—if she'd really wanted to cut him out of the picture, she would and should have done it by now.

Yet Jack was very compelling. Mustering the strength to back out of his arms just before he kissed her hadn't been easy. Now that he'd driven away, she could admit she had wanted that kiss badly. But lord, what would've happened if she'd allowed her hormones to overrule her head?

And what about Wednesday night? she wondered, as she unlocked her apartment door. How was she going to deal with the temptation awaiting her two flights up?

"With outright avoidance, that's how," she muttered aloud, heading straight for the telephone. At this point in her life, she wasn't about to compromise her wishes, her best interests, because Jack Candelaria wouldn't—couldn't—take no for an answer.

She dialed her brother's number. "Charlie, I need an objective second opinion on this business plan I've received. Can we get together at the store to review it? Say after work on Wednesday?"

Chapter Six

Where was Charlie?

Twenty minutes after closing for the day, Mary checked her watch again. Her brother was usually so prompt. Why did he have to be late tonight of all nights? She was eager to busy herself in a discussion of the Michaels' proposal, so her thoughts would stop wandering to a certain someone who was waiting—futilely—for her to show up.

Impatient with waiting, Mary folded a pile of just-tagged outfits over her arm, grabbed an armful of pint-size plastic hangers and headed for the toddlers' racks. She was midway through the size 3Ts when Charlie's call came. "I didn't forget you, Mare—I forgot about Diane's bridge game," he said before Mary had a chance to say hello. "She's having the la-dies at the house, and I've got the kids, who are begging to have supper at Friendly's. You want us to stop by the shop after we eat?''

Mary glanced around the large front room, which she'd spent a better part of the day reorganizing. As much as she loved her nieces, they tended to go crazy over the store's used toys, baby carriages and pretty party dresses. The little sweethearts could make a shambles of this place in minutes. But she didn't want to cancel—not tonight. That left only one viable alternative for the three rambunctious girls.

"Let's meet at my apartment," she told Charlie. "How long do you think supper will take?"

"Forty-five minutes, tops."

She could handle forty-five minutes. By the time she finished hanging the toddler clothes, drove home, changed and made herself a quick dinner, Charlie and the girls should be arriving. If Jack Candelaria should happen to come looking for her, she wouldn't have a moment to spare. This time she'd be prepared to turn him away.

She wasn't prepared, however, for the mouth-watering aromas wafting through the hallways when she arrived at the apartment building. And she knew exactly where they were coming from. Brushing aside what had to be a twinge of guilt, because it couldn't possibly be regret, Mary escaped into her apartment.

No sooner had she pulled on a pair of denim cut-offs and a white T-shirt than there was a knock on her door. She froze until the second knock jerked her into action. Squaring her shoulders, reminding herself to be firm, Mary went to the door to face Jack.

Except it wasn't Jack.

"I've got my tour itinerary for you, Mary," Roberta O'Brien from apartment 2-C announced, "and the phone numbers where I can be reached in case of an emergency."

Relief whooshed through her lungs as she waved the tenant inside. Mary tried to concentrate on Roberta's instructions for taking care of the cat and plants while she was vacationing with her daughter and granddaughter. But through the open door the spicy bouquet of tomato sauce and green peppers simmering was way too distracting.

"Smells good, huh?" Roberta noted.

Nodding, Mary shut the door.

"Would you believe that handsome young man in 3-B has been cooking all afternoon? I was picking up my mail when he came in carrying a bag full of groceries. Said he was having a special guest for dinner."

"Really?" Mary squirmed.

"Oh, he's just the sweetest guy. So I offered to lend him my china and crystal."

"He took you up on it?"

"Sure did. I gave him two full place settings—bread and salad plates included," Roberta revealed. "Then a little later I remembered the white permanent-press tablecloth I picked up on sale at Steigers and thought he might like to use it, too—they wash beautifully, you know."

"I know."

"Anyway, I brought it up to his apartment, and the dear boy was actually vacuuming. Imagine that?"

She didn't dare imagine anything about Jack.

"Well, he was glad for the tablecloth, and then he showed me what he was cooking and the wine he had chosen. I've gotta say, that's some lucky lady he's entertaining tonight." A heavy sigh warbled through her sizable chest, "Oh, if I were thirty years younger..."

Mary's stomach knotted. As the "lucky lady" in question, she was curious. What was Jack doing at this very moment? Opening a bottle of wine? Trying to keep the food warm? Wondering if she was ever coming?

Oh, she wished Charlie would hurry up and get here.

She made a small salad and ate it in an absent-minded daze, caught between praying for Charlie to show up and for Jack not to. Lord, she hated waiting like this. She'd done too much of it in her life: waiting at home in Springfield while Andy went away to college; waiting for special weekends, holidays, summers to see him; waiting to get married until after he finished law school. When Andy broke the engagement, she waited to get into graduate school in Washington, and then ended up waiting for her father to recover from heart surgery so she could leave, then finding it too late. Ever the faithful fiancée and dutiful daughter, she had waited out of a sense of love. Both times she'd ended up losing.

The phone rang and she had a nagging feeling it was Charlie. "Where are you?" she asked as soon as she picked up the receiver.

"We're just finishing now. The waiter was so incredibly slow, you won't believe."

"I believe, Charlie."

"Ah, Mare, we're gonna be delayed just a little longer. Lisa accidentally knocked over her milk shake, and it spilled on Jenny and she's soaked. I've got to take her home to wash and change." Charlie's explanation rose over the giggling, whining and squealing in the background. "But that won't take more than a few minutes. We'll be there before you know it."

Mary expected it would take Charlie a half an hour, at the very least. But her sense of urgency had passed. It was almost seven-thirty; she doubted Jack would come hunting for her now. He must have realized she was not coming for dinner. A pang of guilt sprang anew. She hoped there'd be no hard feelings on Jack's part.

As she took the kitchen wastebasket down the hall to the trash room, the lingering aroma of Jack's cooking was inescapable. Remorse twisted around her heart like coarse twine. The one image she'd been avoiding with a vengeance—of Jack sitting upstairs waiting—flooded her brain. Thinking of the food, the wine, the china, the crystal and Roberta's permanent-press tablecloth made her feel worse. And she hadn't even accepted his invitation! But ignoring him outright like this seemed so cold. Being a well-seasoned player in the waiting game, she couldn't bear to inflict its uncertainty on Jack.

She should tell him, one last time, that she didn't want to get involved. Perhaps Jack would believe her when he saw she'd never intended to join him for dinner. If nothing else, her worn cutoffs and plain T-shirt would back up her disinterest in a romantic dinner à deux. Back in the apartment she dashed off a note to Charlie saying she was up in 3-B and then stuck it on her door.

She wouldn't go in. She'd say her piece and he'd see the way she was dressed—that would be the end of it.

Climbing the stairs, Mary silently intoned this list in her head, over and over, like a sacred mantra. Before she knew it, she was knocking on Jack's door.

He answered it right away.

"Hi," she said with a rasp, her voice deserting her.

Jack's brown eyes lit up and he held her gaze with a smile so warm, it made her heart flutter. Behind him, the apartment lights had been dimmed and candlelight flickered invitingly.

Don't go in!

"I'm sorry about dinner."

He shook his head, answering gently, "Everything's fine now. Come in."

She stood her ground in the hallway. "I thought you would've given up on me by now."

"I told you I like to keep hoping."

Say your piece!

"But the dinner's probably ruined. You shouldn't have waited."

"The dinner kept fine."

"I half expected you to come downstairs looking for me."

"I considered it." His eyes twinkled, yet his smile remained irresistibly welcoming. "But I figured you'd come if you wanted to. And here you are."

"Only to tell you why I'm not having dinner with you."

"No, no, Mary," he said, pulling her inside. "It doesn't work that way."

Show him how badly you're dressed!

But all protest died in her throat when she saw the round, candlelit table, beautifully set for two. The crystal sparkled, the china glistened. But what really snagged her attention was the glass vase of late-summer roses, simply, if not artfully arranged. Somehow, that little vase of home-grown red roses outshone the spit and polish of the table settings. "You picked those yourself?"

He nodded, the shadow from a candle flame dancing across his smooth face. "From my mother's garden."

The notion of him picking flowers—for her—zinged her heart. She didn't know what to say, about the roses, about everything he'd prepared and kept ready. Why hadn't he given up on her, written her off as a no-show? Was he *that* self-confident?

"Would you care for a glass of wine before we eat?" he asked.

Put an end to it!

Declaring she'd already eaten was on the tip of her tongue, but she couldn't bring herself to say it. Hearing about all his preparations from Roberta O'Brien was one thing, having the results staring back at her turned out to be quite another. She shook her head. "Having dinner together would be a mistake."

"How do you know that? Didn't you say you've learned not to count your chickens before they hatch?" He led her to the beige cotton-covered sofa in the middle of the room and sat her down.

Her willpower flagged. Maybe she could stay for one glass of wine, to appease him and her guilt. She was sure Charlie wouldn't show up for at least another twenty minutes.

While Jack went to get the wine in the kitchen, Mary surveyed the combination living and dining room. With the walls painted a fresh off-white, ceilings replastered and the wood floors refinished to a natural blond oak, the room felt airy and clean. She had to smile at the sparse furnishings: the sofa and a comfortable leather reading chair, a few lamps, the round dining table with oak Windsor chairs and no paintings, pictures or bric-a-brac anywhere. It was comfortable enough to suit Jack's temporary needs, yet would be a snap to pack up when he was ready to move.

"You've done a great job fixing up the place so far," she commented, when Jack returned with two glasses of red wine.

"Thanks." He handed her a glass. "Wait until you see the kitchen."

He sat close beside her, his tan slacks brushing her bare thigh. A sliver of shyness wedged its way into her already faltering poise, and she tried to avoid his gaze. Sitting here with him, like this, was different from sitting with him out on the front steps or even at the top of a lovely grassy hill. This was private, intimate... dangerous.

"Did you bring this furniture from your house in Lexington?" she asked, trying, at least, to get control of the conversation.

"No, that's all being sold with the house. This stuff is rented." He glanced around the room. "I've decided to start from scratch when I find a house here in town."

"New furniture for a new life?" she offered, although she thought it sad that he'd sell everything off.

"Yeah, something like that."

"Dad's shown you some properties?"

"Just a couple. We're going out again later in the week."

Mary lifted her glass. "Here's wishing you luck, then."

"Here's wishing us both luck—for the future." He tapped his glass against hers.

Her gaze wandered across the rim of her glass, stealing a look, drinking in his dark, taut handsomeness as she drank the full-bodied wine. Then his eyes met hers, and Mary couldn't say if the sudden, yielding heat coursing through her blood was because of the zinfandel or because of Jack.

As he shifted to face her, his brown eyes captivated her with their liquid brown transluscence. Reaching out, his fingers lifted a length of hair and caressed it. "I would've been awfully disappointed if you hadn't come."

His low voice was as disarming as its message. Yet she managed to eek out some resistance. "But I told you the reason I came. I didn't feel right about letting you sit up here—"

He pressed a finger to her lips. "I don't care what brought you here."

His thumb moved to her cheek, caressing it softly, gently in small circular strokes. Mary sat as if in a trance. Filled with the creamy warmth of anticipation, she hoped for more of his velvet voice and sensuous glances. She couldn't ever remember feeling quite like this before. It was like being under the influence of something both magical and flesh-and-blood real at the same time. The truth was she enjoyed being around Jack and she'd been almost unbearably attracted to him from day one. The time had come to be honest about these feelings, with herself and with him.

She covered his caressing hand with her own. "Guilt's not the real reason I'm here. I came because I couldn't keep away."

"Mary." She watched his chest rise with a slow, deep breath as he looked into her eyes. "I believe we're making progress."

He leaned in close, his eyes locked on hers. His mouth felt feathery light at first, then he deepened the kiss and her lids drifted closed as she drifted into him. He took his time savoring her lips, enveloping her in a whirl of languorous delight. A sigh purred deep inside her throat, but he must've heard because his hand slithered back from her cheek to cup her skull, pressing her closer, harder against his mouth. Her heart pounded in her ears, sounding like the rumble of distant thunder.

The tip of his tongue caressed away every last trace of hesitance until her lips parted and willingly, hungrily, drew his warmth inside. His mouth felt as hot as the noonday sun and tasted like bittersweet wine. Except the sun had never made her dizzy, and she doubted any wine could make her feel as heady as she did now.

She was losing herself in this kiss, riding with excitement in a way she never had before. Not even a low, insistent buzz pulsing in the background made much of a dent in her concentration. This was too good to pull back from or to let go of.

But Jack muttered in frustration before tearing his mouth away. "I've got to turn that damn thing off."

"What is it?" she gasped, her breathing beyond her control.

"The rolls in the oven. I'd better turn it off before they burn." He stood up from the couch. "I'll be right back. Don't move!"

"But your dinner, won't it—"

"It'll keep."

"You haven't eaten."

"Don't worry about it," he called over his shoulder as he disappeared into the kitchen.

Mary struggled to return to her senses. How could she have allowed herself to get so carried away by a kiss? Granted, it was one hell of a kiss. And, heaven help her, her body was ready for more. Yet she knew her head had to prevail, or there was no telling what might happen.

She got to her feet just as Jack returned. She saw the flicker of disappointment in his eyes. "I'm getting too carried away here," she explained.

"So am I, but why fight it?"

"No, this kind of thing isn't me."

"Kissing isn't your kind of thing?" He gave her a skeptical smile.

Feeling herself turn red, she shook her head. "What I meant was hot and heavy is not my style."

He trailed a finger down her bare arm. "Have you ever really given yourself the chance to find out?"

Her skin tingled from his touch, which worried her enough to bolster her resistance. "I don't like to be rushed, okay?"

"Sure, Mary, sure." He stepped back. "Look, the last thing I want is to scare you or make you uncomfortable."

"You didn't scare me, Jack. It's just that I . . . the problem is . . . Well, it's just that I feel too comfortable with you. But that makes me uncomforta—" His gentle chuckling made her pause. "I sound like a blithering idiot, don't I?"

"Nah, you sound like you need dinner. And maybe more wine." He held out his hand. "You want to stay, don't you?"

The devastating appeal of his face thwarted any response but yes. Hooked into his gaze, Mary simply nodded and let him lead her to the table. He held out a chair, made sure she was comfortably settled, refilled her wineglass, told her what was on the menu. And when he left her for the kitchen, she felt like a heel for having already eaten.

She didn't have long to contemplate this conflict before Jack came in with a basket of warm, sweet-smelling rolls and two small plates. When he set one of the plates in front of her, her mood plunged. On it was a beautifully made garden salad.

"Is something wrong?" he asked her from across the table. "Don't you like salad?"

"Oh, Jack, you're gonna hate me. I've been terrible about this whole thing."

Looking puzzled, he said nothing.

"I decided I wasn't going to have dinner with you tonight, and I didn't want to be tempted. So I deliberately ate as soon as I got home."

"You've already eaten?" The letdown in his voice was unmistakable.

"Yes! And look at the way I'm dressed," she announced, standing up. "I thought for sure you'd realize I had no intention of staying for dinner."

Jack's gaze roamed over her T-shirt, along her denim cutoffs and down the length of her legs. A pesky quiver of excitement rippled through her. "I noticed your outfit was on the informal side. But I like it," he added with a flirty smile.

She sank back into the chair. "Ah, Jack, what's worse is I set up an appointment with my brother to discuss the Boston stores—for exactly this time."

Jack flinched. "Then, where is he?"

"Beats me. He must've got hung up after I last spoke with him, or he would've been here by now."

His eyes narrowed. "I see."

"You have every right to be angry with me, you know."

"Angry's too strong. Annoyed is more like it," he declared. "Did you really have to try so hard to avoid having dinner with me? You could've just stayed home."

"Apparently I knew I'd have trouble doing that." She lifted her palms and shrugged. "After all, here I am."

After mulling this over, Jack broke into a slow grin. "If you put it like that, how can I be annoyed?" He captured one of her hands with an affectionate squeeze. "Perhaps extremely flattered is more in line. And grateful that Charlie stood you up."

His smile alone was worth admitting the truth.

"By the way, what did you have for dinner?"

"A salad."

"That's it?" He shook his head. "Think you might have room for a little baked ziti?"

She breathed in deeply. "It smells awfully good."

Releasing her hand, he picked up both salads. "We'll move on to the main course."

Jack returned from the kitchen, a bubbling hot casserole in his mitted hands. They ate and talked and laughed until Mary pushed back from the table. "I'm stuffed."

"Good, because I didn't make it to the bakery for a dessert."

"You mean no homemade dessert?" she teased.

He shrugged. "Truth be known, Mary, baked ziti is the one dish I make well. After this it's hot dogs and canned beans, or overcooked spaghetti."

Mary couldn't help laughing. "That's your traditional Italian upbringing showing. My father couldn't boil water if his life depended on it. And my mother never had Charlie help in the kitchen when we were growing up. Of course, his wife straightened him out after they got married."

"My wife and I were always too busy to spend much time in the kitchen. We lived on take-out and microwaved frozen dinners," he said, as he gathered up the plates and silverware.

He accepted her offer to help with the dishes, warning they'd have to be washed by hand since the dishwasher hadn't been hooked up yet. Mary didn't mind, although she found working in the small alley kitchen a challenge. Moving about its narrow confines without bumping into Jack was tricky, and watching every step only intensified her awareness of him.

"I'll wash, you rinse and we'll let them air dry on the rack," he said. This game plan brought them side by side, shoulders and arms grazing with almost every move. For Mary the proximity was a cross between misery and bliss. After her unrestrained reaction to his kiss, she'd better not act on this enticing closeness.

But, oh, how she wanted to.

Which was all the more reason to stop fantasizing about being wrapped in arms that were now elbow-deep in fluffy white suds. "I'm surprised you don't consider yourself a good cook," she said, hoping this came off as a natural turn of conversation rather than an attempt to distract herself. "The ziti was really delicious."

"I've cooked my share of ziti over the years," he admitted, handing her a plate to rinse. "Actually, before I was married, I'd make it to impress the ladies."

She dunked the dinner plate in the clear water. She couldn't help asking, "Did you want to impress me?"

Turning to her, he curved a wet hand along the sensitive arc of her neck, and a thin trail of soap foam sizzled on her skin. His gaze was piercing and direct. "I think that's obvious."

The dish Mary was holding slipped back into the water. Her gaze latched on to his. She was thirty years old and tired of shoulds and shouldn'ts. She was aching to reach out beyond the expected and safe. Sure, Jack may've been delivering a smooth one about impressing her, but she didn't much care right now. Nor did she care that her hands—wending their way up the front of his shirt—were dripping wet.

When her hands found his shoulders, he pulled her to him. Her eyes widened at the pressure of his muscled chest against her softness, and she could feel his heart beating—almost as fast as hers. The desire in his eyes reflected her own, and she realized denial was no longer possible. He could see the truth for himself.

As Jack lowered his head, her lips trembled in anticipation. With her yearning for him exposed, she knew she was vulnerable, but she felt wildly free. She welcomed his kiss without reservation, drinking up his urgent fire and feeling its liquid heat rush through her.

She felt his wet, hungry hands glide down her body, cupping her left breast. Damp fingers caressed its tip slowly, deliciously, making her moan. He whispered her name in response, kissing her forehead, her eyes, her cheeks. His hand slid down to her bare thigh, but the moist residue of soapy water couldn't cool her fevered skin, couldn't douse the fire in her heart. Jack reclaimed her mouth and she gave herself up to the sheer sensation of it.

The knock on the door came as a jolt. Jack stiffened slightly in her arms—but only for a moment. He resumed his caressing. "Ignore it—" he breathed between kisses "—they'll go away."

Mary was only too happy to acquiesce. But a second, louder knock ensued. "Jack? Anybody home?"

Startled, she pushed away from Jack. "It's Charlie. He's looking for me."

"Don't worry. I'll take care of it."

"You can't do that." She followed him to the door.

"Hey, Charlie, what can I do for you?" Jack asked after opening the door partway.

"I'm looking for Mary. The note on her door said she's up here."

Mary stepped out from behind Jack. Although she avoided looking at him, she felt his less-than-welcoming stare. "Where have you been, Charlie?"

"I'm sorry, Mare, but when we got to the house, the bridge ladies spent forever oohing and ahhing over the kids, and then Jenny couldn't find anything clean to change into. I phoned to tell you we were still running behind, but you didn't answer," he explained. "By then the baby was fussing, so Diane insisted I put her down for the night. And you know how long that can take."

Not in a generous frame of mind, Mary just rolled her eyes. So Charlie looked to Jack.

"Sounds like a tough night, pal," commented Jack.

Charlie turned to her and was about to say something, when he looked back at Jack and then at Mary again. She realized he'd finally noticed their slightly disheveled, slightly damp state. Charlie coughed nervously. "Did I interrupt something?"

"Well, actually—"

"Nothing, actually," she snapped quickly, glaring at Jack. "We were just talking."

Jack did not look pleased. "Ah, Charlie, could you excuse us for a second?"

"Sure, I'll be right here."

Jack pulled her out to the kitchen. "Charlie realizes he's shown up at a bad time. He'll understand and leave." He drew her to him. "I'll explain to him."

"No, you won't," she protested, although the warmth of his body close to hers was eliciting a different response.

"Don't worry, I'll be discreet."

"That's not what I'm worried about." Her halfhearted attempt to pull away was no match for his embrace. "I can't just kiss Charlie off, not after all the trouble he had getting here."

Jack held her away from him, his grip on her shoulders gentle, but firm. "I thought you'd want to stay."

"He came to review the business plan for the Boston stores." She shrugged his arms away. "And right now that takes priority over everything else."

"I thought you hauled Charlie over here to help keep you away from me."

Mary clenched her fist in indignation. Even though what he said was true—partially—the arrogance of his reminder vexed her. "I need to discuss the business plan with Charlie. The Michael sisters are waiting to hear from me."

"Is one more day going to make a difference?" His voice was tinged with impatience.

"You're missing the point, Jack." The expectant expression on his face made her resent him all the more. Where did he get off acting like this, anyway? A few kisses didn't bind her to him, for heaven's sake.

Charlie called from the next room. "Could you guys hurry it up? Leesy and Jenny are waiting downstairs."

She turned away from Jack. "Look, I've got to go."

"Mary, I want you to stay."

The tone of his voice stopped her. He hadn't demanded, but requested. Her resistance waffled for a moment, until Mary reminded herself who she was dealing with. Yes, Jack had indeed issued a request—a typically selfish one.

She met his gaze. "I need to see to my family and my business."

As she spoke, the clamor of little girls running and giggling resounded in the hall. "What's taking you so long, Daddy?" Lisa, the oldest, called. "Where's Auntie Mary?"

Resignation shadowed Jack's face. He moved away from the kitchen door. "Goodbye, Mary," he said with a finality that brooked no response. "Thanks for coming."

Chapter Seven

Jack shut the apartment door firmly, not knowing who he was more angry with, Mary or himself. How could she take off the way she did, when she did? Granted, he may have been a little overbearing there at the end, but dammit, she'd turned positively pig-headed.

Yet it was his own fault for letting it get to this point. Right from the start Mary had made no bones about what she wanted and where she was headed. He knew her goals didn't mesh with his. But something about her had thrown off his perspective, causing him to disregard one of the sadder lessons of his life. Maybe it was her inherent warmth, maybe the way she laughed, maybe the way she made him laugh.

Heading back to the kitchen, his gaze fell on the roses. He thought about the look in Mary's eyes when she'd first spotted them—kind of glittery with appreciation. That had been when he'd decided to give her the roses to take home, as a memento of what had—at that point—looked to be a promising evening.

"So much for promising evenings," he muttered, picking up the glass vase and continuing to the kitchen. He plunked it down on the counter next to the dishes he and Mary hadn't gotten around to washing. Because of the kisses.

Lord, he could still feel her wet hands curving around his neck and her slick fingers dancing on his skin. Her mouth had been warm and welcoming, her body so soft and yielding in his arms. A fresh jolt of desire roiled through him. Mary had been right there with him, no hesitation, no backing away from the excitement building between them. Whether she liked it or not, she'd wanted him. Until Charlie had shown up, that is.

"Damn!" He slammed his fist on the counter. The pile of dirty dishes clinked in response.

Yet Jack knew it was pointless to let this interlude with Mary get the better of him. It had turned out to be one of those instant attractions that makes a man think he's nuts about a woman when, in actuality, he'd been just plain nuts. Best to chalk the whole thing up to temporary insanity and get on with the life he came back to build. He needed Mary Piletti messing up his plans like he needed a hole in the head.

"So much for you guys." Jack lifted the roses from the vase and chucked them into the trash.

Within two days Jack had thrown himself into house-hunting with a vengeance. He'd spent a better part of a day studying the stack of property listings Mario Piletti had sent over. But when Mario took him to see his selections the following morning, none of them appealed to him.

"We'll keep looking," Mario assured him, as they drove away from a nondescript rambler near the Springfield-Wilbraham town line. "New listings come up on the computer all the time."

"The sooner the better as far as I'm concerned." After the incident with Mary the other night, Jack felt a need to get back on track, to get himself firmly reestablished in his hometown.

Mario glanced at him from the passenger seat. "What's the matter? Apartment life getting you down already?"

"Something like that."

"I could show you one more place," he suggested. "Mary says it's a white elephant, and with you being single and all, I didn't think you'd be interested. But it's on the way back to my office. Want to take a look?"

"Sure, why not?" Jack agreed as he turned onto Route 20. "They're not expecting me back at the shop until after one, anyway."

Although this trip had not been fruitful, Jack had enjoyed spending time with the older man. He'd known Mario for most of his life, but only as his father's good friend and the Piletti kids' dad. Of course, Mario was a lot grayer now, and he seemed even more diminutive than Jack remembered. But he still had that no-nonsense manner that had often shushed Peek Street gossips and kept the more rambunctious neighborhood kids in line. A trait he'd passed on to his only daughter, Jack thought with a scowl.

Now, as an adult and a client, Jack recognized Mario as a businessman of the old school: dedicated, straightforward, and again, no-nonsense. In that regard, Mario reminded him of his own father. There the similarity ended, however, because Mario was doing the one thing Vito never could: accept him as a grown man.

"All right, now take the next left and then the first right," Mario directed. Jack recognized the streets, and when Mario pointed out the house, he recognized it, too.

"The Feeney place is for sale?"

Mario nodded. "Sally's getting on these days."

"I used to mow the lawns for her when I was a kid."

"Then you know the house."

"No, she would never let me inside, not even to use the bathroom. She said healthy boys like me were perfectly capable of going behind the bushes."

Mario burst into laughter. "Her father said the same thing to me when I mowed here. Can you believe it?"

"You think she'll let me in now?" Jack joked as they got out of the car.

"Not a problem today. She's gone on an all-day mystery bus ride with her Golden Age club. You can look at the entire house to your heart's content."

He doubted he'd give the house more than a cursory once-over. It was much bigger than anything he had in mind. Standing behind Mario as he fiddled with the front door lockbox, Jack couldn't help admiring the design and solid craftsmanship of the place. Even faded and peeling yellow paint didn't detract from its appeal. Inside on the main floor, the rooms, though large and high ceilinged, were darkened by heavy draperies. The furniture was good but worn, as was everything else from wallpaper to carpets. The huge kitchen was state-of-the-art—circa 1959. Mario followed him upstairs, keeping a few steps behind, saying little except to point out an interesting feature here and there.

After looking through all the rooms, Jack found himself returning to the master bedroom. Although reeking of Sally Feeney's floral toilet water and overdone in cabbage rose chintz, it was a wonderful room with a fireplace and a big bay window overlooking the backyard garden. He hoped whoever bought this place would yank down those drapes and let the light shine in as it was meant to.

Mario came up behind him. "You like it, don't you?"

"Sure I do," he said, shrugging. "I've got a thing for old houses. The one I'm selling in Lexington was built in 1772. Renovating it was practically my avocation."

"Then this place is right up your alley. Mary thinks it needs a lot of fixing up."

"She's seen it?" Had she liked it, too, he wondered?

"Not since she was a kid, but she remembers it. I think she has a thing for old houses—just like you."

Is that so, Mario?

"At least old Sally let her in," Jack said, smiling as he sauntered out of the room.

"Maybe I should bring her over to see it again sometime," Mario continued, as they walked down the wide, elegant staircase. "You know, when she was little she would come preview listings with me all the time."

Jack didn't comment. Mary was the one person he didn't want to talk about.

When they reached the front door, Mario paused for a sweeping glance of the main floor. "What do you say, Jack? Interested?"

"It's a great house—but not for me."

Outside, Jack waited by the car while Mario locked everything up. When the older man returned, he was shaking his head.

"They don't make 'em like that anymore. You know, it'd be a wonderful place to raise a great big family."

Jack felt himself wince. "I'm too old to have a 'great big family'—big enough for that house, anyway."

"Ah, you're just a youngster," Mario scoffed. "Of course, it's always sad when a man your age loses a wife, but God's a giver of second chances. Keep an open mind. You never know, another woman might come along when you least expect it."

"That's true, you never know." Nice try, Mario.

As Jack made a move toward the car, Mario leaned back against the driver's door and pulled a clean handkerchief from his jacket pocket. He took off his eyeglasses and began rubbing them with the white cloth. "I hope you don't mind me mentioning this," he began, trying—and not succeeding—to sound casual, "but one of my granddaughters told me Mary had dinner at your apartment the other night. This true?''

The old man just wouldn't quit, Jack thought, marveling at his tenacity. Figuring there was no point in lying, he nodded his head.

Mario's thin lips lifted into a smile of satisfaction. ''Good. That's very good.''

Mario was so pleased Jack didn't have the heart to tell him that there'd be no more dinners for Mary and himself. He suspected Mario wasn't thrilled that Mary had her heart set on striking out on her own. And, as Mario held the same values as the rest of the old-timers on Peek Street, he probably worried—perpetually—about his unmarried and childless thirty-year-old daughter. Jack would bet the shop on it.

Well, he was not the answer to an old man's prayers.

He had to get Mario off the subject of Mary. Fortunately he didn't have to think hard about how. Since his return to Springfield, he'd been hoping to approach Mario about another matter close to home. Resting his elbow on the car roof, he turned to Mario. ''I want to talk to you about my brother.''

''Peter? What about him?''

''I can't get anywhere with him,'' Jack admitted. ''It's like we're strangers.''

With a deep sigh, Mario put his glasses on. ''He's not happy you're back, that's for sure. But, as far as I can tell, nothing much makes him happy these days.''

''That's what I don't understand, Mario. He's got a great wife, three beautiful kids, a good job with you. Sure he's had his disappointments. But haven't we all?''

"Peter's a good man at heart, and I believe you are, too, Jack." Mario folded his arms across his chest, shaking his head. "But your father, God rest his soul, didn't do you two boys any favors. His unforgiving stubbornness made it impossible for you to come back home and for Peter to ever leave. When you left, Vito made it known he had only one son and one son was all he needed. Pretty hard for a fourteen-year-old to measure up to, wouldn't you say?"

An aching memory, submerged long ago, clutched at Jack's throat. "I didn't plan to stay away all these years...I..."

"Of course you didn't, son." Mario gave his shoulder a sympathetic pat. "And Peter's no fool. He'll come around."

"I wish I could believe that, Mario, I—" He struggled to swallow back the old pain. "He used to really look up to me when we were kids. We were close. Now I hardly know him."

"He's worked for me close to ten years now, so I know him pretty well. He's smart like your father and almost as stubborn," Mario added with a sly wink. "But he's a natural salesman, our top producer."

"Then he's doing well?"

"As well as he can with our small firm. But he's capable of more and he knows it, which I think is the root of his problem. You see, I can't really do any more for him—the business belongs to my son now."

"Could he go out on his own?"

"I've encouraged him to do that for years. Heaven knows there's more than enough business to go around."

"So why hasn't he?"

Mario squinted at him through his spectacles, as if to say the answer was obvious. And when Jack stopped to think about it, he realized it was. "The grocery."

"He blames himself for its failure, even though your mother and I, Gina, Charlie and who knows who else have tried to tell him otherwise." Mario held out his arms in a gesture of hopelessness. "Maybe you should try."

He knew Mario had added that only as an after-thought, but Jack latched on to it. This estrangement had to end. And perhaps he knew a way to accomplish that.

His spirits lifting with hope, he gave the old man a thoughtful smile. "Maybe I will, Mario."

Unable to get Peter out of his mind, Jack dropped by his mother's house right after work. Before he reached the front door he could hear the baby howling. When he let himself in, he found chaos.

Gina, his sister-in-law, was pacing the length of the front hall with baby Elizabeth, trying to sooth her red-faced wails. In the den, his two nephews wrestled in front of the blaring TV, bickering over who got to watch what next.

"Welcome to the zoo," Gina greeted over Elizabeth's cries.

"Guess I came at a bad time," he said, feeling awkward. Gina looked absolutely beat as she rocked the baby in her arms, and the baby looked in pain. "Is she sick?"

"She's teething, poor thing. I was up with her all last night and now—" An angry shout cut her short.

"I'm gonna break your arm if you change that channel!"

"Mommy! Jimmy won't let me watch the Turtles."

"You two stop it this minute or I'll send you to your room."

He was sure the boys hadn't heard her over the racket, and it probably wouldn't have made a difference if they had. Gina rolled her eyes in frustration. Sensing she was at the end of her rope, Jack marched into the den, turned off the TV and sent the boys outside to play. Meanwhile, his mother had returned from a shopping errand.

"Now give me the baby and you go rest. I'll put some of that medicine on her gums, too," she was telling Gina when Jack came back in. "And what are you doing here, Jackie?"

"I'm looking for Peter, actually."

"He's working late tonight. Again." With obvious exasperation, Gina handed Rose the baby. "He's showing houses to two different couples."

His mother shooed Gina upstairs, promising to feed the kids and put them to bed. "Don't worry," she said over her daughter-in-law's protests, "Jackie will help me with the boys."

It wasn't how he'd planned to spend his evening, but, mumbling in agreement, he followed his mother to the kitchen. After Rose applied a foul-looking liquid to Elizabeth's gums, she quieted down, finally. Then Rose held the baby out to him. "Here, take her while I start supper."

He glanced nervously about the room. "Ah, can't you put her in the carriage or something?"

"And have her start crying again?"

"Ma, I'm not used to babies."

"Well, you're back now, so get used to them. Now sit down at the table and I'll hand her to you." Jack did as he was told, though his arms fumbled a bit when he took Elizabeth. Rose chuckled. "Don't worry, she won't break."

The baby felt much sturdier than he'd expected, and softer and warmer, too. He relaxed a little. Elizabeth gazed up at him with wondrous blue eyes, a tad sleepy but curious about this new person holding her. She also seemed to be fishing for a smile, and she got it.

"What did you come to see Peter about?" Rose asked, as she rummaged through the refrigerator.

"Business," he answered, still keeping a watchful eye on the bundle in his arms. "I've got some money to invest, and I thought he might be interested in opening his own real estate office."

"You've got that kind of money?"

He shrugged. "I did well on the stock market in the eighties, like a lot of people." Except I managed to hold on to it, he added silently.

"That's wonderful, and it's wonderful you want to help your brother. But maybe you should wait awhile before bringing it up."

"Why? Don't you think he wants his own business?"

"Not that he'd be willing to admit. Not now. He has to get used to having you back, and get to know you again," Rose explained. "Besides, Peter and Gina are both under a lot of pressure because he works so much. And having me living here with them can't be easy."

"Seems to me you made Gina's evening a whole lot easier just now."

"Oh, this is one of those awful, awful days young mothers have from time to time," his mother insisted. "Gina can manage well enough on her own. And young couples need privacy."

"Look, Ma, when I buy a house here, you can come live with me." But Rose shook her head as she began peeling carrots over the sink. "I really mean it," he added, feeling compelled to say so.

"You're good to ask, but I've had enough of living with my kids. Old ladies need privacy, too." She gave him a stern you-should-know-better look. "Besides, I have plans."

"You do? Are you going to share them with me?"

She dropped the peeler in the sink, then wiped her hands on a dish towel. Her eyes brightened with excitement. "I want to buy an apartment in this new retirement complex they're building off Boston Road." Rose came to the table and sat down. "It's within walking distance of Peek Street, and several people from the neighborhood are buying. Mario Piletti's been helping me."

"It sounds great, but do you have enough money?"

"Mario thinks so. Your father left a couple of small insurance policies that I've never touched." She shot him a teasing smile. "Besides, now I have a rich son, who I'm sure will help out his poor mother if she comes up short."

"You can count on it." He smiled, gratified that his mother would want his help and glad that he was in a position to give it.

"Oh, look at the baby!" His mother cooed. "See, you're a natural."

He looked down at Elizabeth, sound asleep in his arms, oblivious to the world. It felt so strange to have such a small creature curled softly against him, perfectly still and perfectly contented. Strange, but nice.

"So, Jackie, what have you been doing with yourself lately?" Rose inquired out of the blue. "And when are you going to bring Mary Piletti by again?"

"After what happened the last time, I don't think she's in any hurry to come back, Ma."

Rose dismissed this with a wave of her hand. "She understands about Angie."

"We'll see then." Saying anything else would only encourage her, and he didn't want to talk about Mary.

His mother stood up and went to the stove. "Gina has a bag of the boys' clothes she's been planning to take to Mary's store. Poor thing's been too busy to get out. Maybe you could drop it off for her tomorrow?"

If he didn't know better, he'd swear that his mother and Mario Piletti and even baby Elizabeth were conspiring to force him to think of Mary. The trouble was they didn't have to. She'd been a constant presence in his thoughts, brushed aside often, never completely dismissed. Yet in his anger he'd convinced himself that this interest or fascination—whatever—would pass.

But today the frequent mention of her name had simply unleashed his desire to see her. Which was crazy. Usually when he set his mind to something— like staying away from a woman—he stuck to it. With Mary's sweet eyes and sexy smile, that wasn't so easy. He'd encountered a certain loneliness in returning to this place where only his mother was glad to have him back. Yet with Mary...with Mary, he never felt lonely or alienated.

And there was no sense denying that he wanted her. He did. Badly. Touching her, kissing her, feeling how responsive she could be in his arms had ignited a yearning to know more of her soul, to taste more of her passion. Did he really think he could suppress that kind of desire for long? Hadn't Sandra's death taught him that time was too precious to waste? He, of all people, couldn't afford to waste any more time on resentment and prideful anger.

Figuring he was either the biggest fool on earth, or just eminently practical, Jack agreed to take Gina's bag of clothes to Mary's store. He'd go to Mary, seek her out, even pursue her if he had to, and—heaven help him—let the chips fall where they may.

Chapter Eight

"Mary, Jack's here to see you."

Mary dragged her gaze from the column of numbers on the computer screen to focus on her sister-in-law. She felt fuzzy-eyed and wasn't sure she'd heard Diane correctly. "Jack?"

"Jack Candelaria. He's waiting out front to see you."

Her fingers froze on the keyboard. Jack was the last person she expected to show up at her store, especially after what had happened the other night. "Ah, I need a minute to finish this up." She nodded at the screen. "Tell him I'll be right out."

Why was he here? she wondered, as she tapped a few keys quickly to close the file. Three days of silence and now this? He'd been angry that night, very angry. She'd seen it in his eyes, so she was certain that was the end of that. In fact, she had decided it was the end because of the arrogance and selfishness underlining his bid for her to stay. He'd acted like her needs and her wishes were subordinate to his.

She'd been thoroughly annoyed with him then. But now...now she wasn't feeling quite so indignant. The extent of his offense and her resentment had become blurred, helped, no doubt, by how she relived his kisses in her mind countless times a day. She hadn't exactly been living like a nun in the years since Andy broke their engagement, but no kiss in memory came close to matching Jack's.

And now he was here.

Grabbing the hairbrush from her purse, she checked herself out in the full-length mirror hanging on the back of the office door. Trying to calm the sudden flutter in her stomach, she bent forward and brushed her hair vigorously. It fell full and soft around her neck when she stood up to straighten her jade green cotton sweater and navy slacks. She thought she looked okay, but she still felt nervous, and she had no idea what to expect.

Out on the floor she spotted Jack immediately, looking gorgeous and out of place among racks of snowsuits and Brownie uniforms. She noticed he was attracting curious, if not outright admiring glances from her noon-hour customers. She couldn't blame them. When her own heart started doing jumping jacks, she realized she'd missed him—arrogance and all. Which was ridiculous. She should be wary, distant, cool—not utterly glad to see him.

"Hi, Jack."

He turned to her, his brown eyes as warm as coffee when he smiled, and right away, she knew there'd be no pretense between them. Holding back not one iota of the pleasure she felt, Mary returned the smile.

"I brought these boys' clothes from Gina." He held up a large white plastic bag. "I know I could've left them outside your apartment, but I wanted to see your store."

"I see." She took the bag from him. "So, what do you think of it?"

"It's quite the place." His gaze scanned the large main room. "I can honestly say I've never seen anything like it."

Two squealing preschoolers suddenly whisked by them, headed for the brightly decorated play corner she'd set aside for customers' children.

Mary chuckled. "I imagine you haven't."

Showing him around the store, she explained how she color coded and tagged each item by season and consignor number. Jack expressed amazement at the variety of merchandise she carried, especially when he spotted the soccer shoes and ice skates. She was pleased when he remarked on the quality of the inventory, because she'd always prided herself on that.

"When I saw those little T-shirts in your apartment that first afternoon, I certainly didn't envision anything like this," he told her. "It's really impressive."

His enthusiasm made her smile. Jack had to be the most vital man she'd ever met. While the strength of his lean, firm body stirred her pulses, his potent inner essence sparked a different kind of yearning deep inside her. She knew this particular allure had nothing to do with charm and went beyond charisma. No, it was his energy, his drive that she found so compelling and that, perhaps, she craved to possess for herself.

They came back to the front of the store, stopping just outside her office door. "Thanks again for bringing the clothes by. Tell Gina I'll mail her a receipt as soon as I tag these."

Jack took a deep breath. "Look, that's not the only reason I came. I wanted to see you."

"You did?" She felt sure she was grinning like a fool. "I'm glad."

"Would you like to go to a movie with me tonight?"

She was taken aback. "Just like that? What about the other night?"

"What about it?" he shot back and then sighed. "Mary, if we keep hashing out what happened last week or what may happen next month, we're going to lose the chance to just be together. And that would be sad."

He'd get no argument from her, she agreed on both counts.

"All right," she said, lifting her gaze to his, "pick me up at seven?"

Mary gave in to restlessness and honked her car horn. Jack had told her he'd be right out, but she'd been waiting in front of the bike shop for at least fifteen minutes. In the week and a half since he had shown up at Twice as Nice, they had gotten together almost every day, and not once had he been late. She certainly hoped nothing was wrong now. Still she wished Jack would hurry it up; she was starving.

When at last he emerged from the shop, Mary noted that he'd thrown a crisp navy blue blazer over his open-collared shirt and tan slacks. She couldn't take her eyes off him as he locked the shop door and trotted over to the driver's side of the car. Although he appeared fine, something about his expression seemed off. Or was it her imagination?

Popping his head through the open window, he plunked a kiss on her left cheek. "Sorry to be so long. Got a last-minute phone call," Jack explained. "You driving?"

"When it's my treat, I drive."

"Fair enough." He walked over to the passenger side and got in. "So where are you taking me?"

She peered over the rim of her sunglasses. "I told you before, it's a surprise."

"I know, I know. But surprises make me antsy."

"Be patient," she said, as she backed out of the parking lot. "It won't be long."

"Have I been there before?"

She smiled, amused by his boyish curiosity. "You probably have. But not recently."

"That could be any place in this town."

"Sure could."

As she maneuvered through the rush-hour traffic, their lighthearted banter drifted into silence. It felt a little odd. Conversation had flowed so freely between them, seemingly nonstop at times. They talked about their stores, their customers, their parents, growing up on Peek Street, the upcoming city elections, their taste in books and music—he was into sci-fi, she preferred biographies—she adored classic rock, he was tired of it. And much more. She was fascinated by what he thought and had to say, and apparently Jack felt the same way about her.

Yet her prospective business plans, Boston and the Michael sisters were never mentioned, as if they'd both made a silent pledge not to discuss anything so portentous as the future. The possible consequences of this avoidance hovered in the back of her mind, but she didn't care to ponder them too closely. Not these days, anyway. She was having too good a time.

She glanced over at Jack, sitting right beside her yet miles away in thought. Something was on his mind, something troubling, and she didn't know what to do about it. Should she ask what's wrong and offer a sympathetic ear? Or would he consider that an intrusion? Would he rather be left alone? Mary wasn't sure. These very questions, however, made her aware of something important. Despite the concentrated amount of time she and Jack had spent together recently, and despite all that talking, an essential part of him remained unknown to her.

"Oh, my God, it's the Lakeside House!" Jack recognized the old favorite family restaurant the moment she drove into the parking lot. "I thought it had closed down years ago."

"It had. But a local couple who—like us—used to come here as children bought the property and reopened it earlier this summer," she explained. "Except it's not geared to families anymore. They've put in a cocktail lounge, and I heard they've hired a young hotshot chef."

"Ah, I see, fine dining for us nostalgic baby boomers."

"You've got it," she said, happy to see his mood lighten.

The huge old white house, sparkling with fresh paint, looked just as she remembered it. Inside the restaurant, though, she could see extensive renovations had been done. It was airy and open with lots of polished wood and windows. But when the hostess seated them on the greatly expanded glassed-in porch overlooking the lake, she noticed that the best part of the old Lakeside House had been returned to its former funky grandeur.

The lawn beneath the porch sloped gently down to the calm water, where gaily painted footbridges curved across two or three jutting inlets, Adirondack chairs and tables were interspersed along the grassy shoreline, and colorful Japanese lanterns hung above them. As dusk was only now approaching, several ducks still floated close to shore in hopeful anticipation of tossed crumbs.

"Well, what do ya know," Jack murmured, "it looks exactly the same."

After a waiter took their drink order, they strolled down to the lake, reminiscing about when they had come here as children with their families. As they walked along the water's edge, a male and female mallard swam up close to beg with low, nagging quacks.

"Sorry, pals," Jack called, holding out his empty hands when the quacking grew more insistent. Another guest meandered over with some crackers, so the mallards turned tail on Mary and Jack.

Mary winked at him. "Don't worry, they'll be back."

Smiling, he led her toward some chairs. "Feeding the ducks was always the best part about this place—after the huge desserts, that is. My Dad would always wrap the leftover rolls in a napkin before the waitress snatched the breadbasket away. Then he'd hand them under the table to Peter and me, and we'd run down here to feed the ducks. Once Peter got carried away and wound up knee-deep in water, ruining his good Sunday shoes. Boy, did I catch it for that."

"You? Why?"

"Because I was older and should've been looking out for him." His tone echoed the merriment in his eyes. "Since you've never been an older brother, you couldn't possibly understand."

"But I have an older brother. And whenever he got stuck taking the blame for me, he'd find a way to make me pay."

"You can be sure I extracted my revenge, too." His mouth curved into a crafty grin as the waiter appeared with their drinks.

This minor interruption somehow quashed Jack's high spirits, and again he slipped away into a contemplative silence. Saying nothing, she studied his profile as he gazed out at the lake, apparently lost in thought. Lost in memories, too? She wondered if difficulties with his family had been the reason for his earlier silence in the car.

Had the Lakeside House been the wrong choice for tonight?

The breeze off the water fluttered through his chocolate brown hair, and she wanted nothing more than to sit on his lap, brush the mussed locks from his forehead and coax him to share with her what was on his mind. After all, they had talked of so many things before.

As if he'd read her mind, he looked over at her and caught her staring. She thought she saw a flicker of pain in his dark eyes, but then it was gone, shuttered away from her with a swiftness that left her reeling. Again she realized there was much she didn't know about Jack. But this time the realization wagged a finger of caution at her yen to soothe and comfort him: beware of getting in too deep.

"Shall we go up and order dinner?" he asked. "I seem to remember you muttering something about being starved, when you picked me up."

"I was—I am." The excitement of being with Jack and coming here to Lakeside had distracted her. "Especially now that you've reminded me. One of my customers told me the veal Marsala is to die for."

Jack curved his arm about her waist, and they walked slowly up the hill. At the crest, before they went inside the restaurant, he glanced down at the shoreline. "I wonder if Peter's been back here yet."

"I don't know," she answered gently, having caught the wistfulness in his voice. It seemed her intuition had been correct. His family—or his brother, at least—was on his mind tonight. Her heart went out to him, and any notion of remaining detached flew out the window.

"Maybe we could invite Peter and Gina to come here with us sometime," she suggested, as they found their table. "I think it'd be fun."

"Sweetheart, if you can get my brother to acknowledge my existence, more power to you," Jack said, sitting across from her, "because he won't even return my phone calls."

After the waiter took their order, Mary listened to Jack explain his wish to help Peter open his own real estate business. "My mother thinks I should wait before broaching the idea to him. So I thought I could mend some fences by spending time with him, go bike riding, have lunch, play ball with him and his boys— anything! But he's been impossible to reach. I have half a mind to plunk myself down at your father's office and stay there until he shows up."

Impatience and frustration seemed to literally coil through his body, as he hunched closer to tell her more about his intentions and Peter's roadblocks. She really felt for Jack. Coming home to Peek Street had been loaded with emotional land mines, and she realized Jack never knew what might trigger another explosion. She was sorry it was difficult for him. But after his earlier moody silences, she felt gratified that he was opening up to her.

"Jack, I hope you follow Rose's advice to wait," she said. "I've heard my father say more than once that pride is Peter's strength and his weakness. Don't expect him to jump at your offer the first time you suggest it. Because, no matter how wonderful, how 'no strings' it is, Peter's going to deal with it in his own way, in his own time."

"I know this up here." He tapped a finger to his forehead. "But what I feel I should do is grab him by the shoulders and shout, 'Time passes too fast. Let's get on with the rest of our lives.'" Impatience smoldering in his eyes, he shook his head. "I guess coming here tonight reminded me how close he and I used to be. And how far we have to go to get back there."

"The Lakeside probably wasn't the best place to bring you—with the memories it holds. I'm sorry," she said. "It didn't occur to me that—"

"No, it *is* the best place. Really," he insisted, reaching across the table to clasp her hands between his. "Remembering the good times is better than dwelling on the acrimony between us. Now I'm convinced that I have to keep trying—no matter how long it takes. Somehow I'm gonna get through his thick skull."

"Are you sure you're okay?" A vague uneasiness still needled her. "You seemed distracted even before we got here. And down at the lake just now, you seemed miles away."

Jack looked at her with speculative eyes, as if he were debating with himself about how best to respond. Then his hands closed tighter around hers. "I'm sorry, Mary. It was the phone call."

"The one you had while I was waiting outside the store?"

He nodded. "From my attorney in Boston. The sale of my house is going to settlement soon, so we had to discuss the details of signing my rights to Sandra's estate over to her father and sister."

She was puzzled. "You're signing away what your wife left you?"

"Considering the circumstances, she should've left everything to her family, anyway. Not me."

What circumstances? she wondered, although she didn't feel she should ask. "It must be difficult deciding what to do in those kinds of situations," she said instead.

"I figured it was probably what Sandra would've preferred. She did extremely well in business over the years. It just seemed right that her family benefit from her success." He shrugged his shoulders. "But the phone call did throw me. The door's closing on that part of my life. Feels strange."

And sad, too, she suspected. "Now I understand why you were so quiet earlier."

"Yeah, that was it," he admitted. "But I've got to let the past go, and being with you tonight helps a lot." He gave her a smile that just about stopped her heart.

Fortunately the waiter arrived with their food, which forced her to do something other than stare at Jack's handsome face. While they ate, she looked about the restaurant, picking out familiar architectural details remaining from the old Lakeside days and finding exciting new features from the recent renovation. What intrigued her most was a bandstand and small dance floor located close to the new cocktail lounge. She asked the waiter about it when she paid the check.

"There's dancing here on Friday and Saturday nights," the waiter revealed. "The bands vary from all kinds of rock and roll to swing and slow dancing."

"You like to dance?" Jack asked when the waiter left.

"It's not something I do very often, but yeah, I like to."

"Then I'll have to bring you back when there's a band—as long as it's not one that plays classic rock," he added with a twinkle in his eye.

That was all right with her. With Jack, she had something more like slow dancing in mind, for it would be an acceptable, noncommittal and delightful way to get what she'd been longing for all week: to be held in Jack's arms.

In the past week and a half, the physical contact between her and Jack had amounted to nothing more intense than occasional tender kisses and affectionate cuddles. There'd been no return to the stunning, passionate kisses they'd shared in his apartment. For reasons of his own, Jack was deliberately holding back. She felt the tension in him when he drew near, and she sensed the battle he was waging within himself each time he curtailed a kiss or eased away from an embrace. Although this limited physical contact took some pressure off, it also left her craving more of him.

How could he be so constant and unyielding when she was beside herself with wanting him?

And there lay the irony, because she knew she could do something about it. A signal of her desire. A whisper of her need. That's all it would take; it would be so easy. But giving into the temptation would be akin to opening a Pandora's box of problems for her and Jack. She feared getting in too deep with him, caught up in more than she bargained for, or worse, stuck where she didn't want to be. These apprehensions baffled her at times. How could she be so drawn to this man, yet be so torn by doubt?

She had no answer, and until she did, she would gladly accept the existing state of affairs: conversations that exhilarated and often made her laugh, kisses and caresses that warmed her, but led nowhere. Sure, she was frustrated, but she was also happy.

Of course, she realized as she drove Jack back to his store after dinner, the situation between them was transitory at best. Something would have to give. How long would he stand for this? How long could she take it? How long would she even be around? But as Jack watched her drive, his smile illuminated by the glowing beam of oncoming traffic, she didn't want to dwell on what was to come. Because, for the first time in her life, right now was the best possible place to be.

Chapter Nine

Letting go of the last remnants of sleep, Mary fumbled through the bedclothes to reach the ringing telephone. Lorna Michael's voice, apologizing for calling so early, snapped her awake. "Mary, we were so pleased with your suggestions for the new stores. In fact, we really need to sit down and talk. How soon can you come to Boston?"

"How soon do you need me?"

"Tomorrow if possible. A wonderful location in Brookline has become available, but if we want it we'll have to act fast," Lorna explained. "Also, there's a good chance we can work out a great deal on a second location with the same landlord. We need you to come see them. And our lawyer says we should get on the ball and start formalizing things between us, so you should plan on staying several days."

This was what she'd been waiting for—she could feel her creative juices stirring already. Suddenly her head was full of questions about the locations and their layouts, time projections, everything. She couldn't wait to get to Boston. "It'll take me the better part of today to square away everything here. But I can probably drive out tonight and meet you first thing tomorrow morning."

Excited, Mary scrambled out of bed, put on some coffee and rang up Jack's apartment. She had to tell someone about the call, and there was no one better to talk with than Jack. After numerous unanswered rings, she gave up, concluding he must've left for work early. Disappointed, she decided she'd try to catch up with him later in the morning.

In the rush of arranging extra help for the store and getting Lou Ponzini to keep an eye on the apartment building, plus the banking and myriad other tasks she had to do before leaving town, time got away from her. It was well into the afternoon before she got a chance to stop by the bicycle shop to see Jack. When she arrived, the place was humming with preweekend business.

"Good afternoon, Miss Piletti. Here to see Jack?" asked Fred, from behind the checkout counter.

"If he's not too busy."

"Never too busy for you, I imagine," he said with a senior citizen's knowing glint. "He's back in children's bikes."

Mary walked between two high racks of athletic clothing to the rear of the store. She could hear Jack speaking. "Let's see, we've got baby pink, hot pink, neon green, electric blue and sky blue. Yellow and white, too. What's your favorite color, Alison?''

Mary peeked around the end rack. "Hot pink!" A little girl crowed, her blond ponytail bobbing behind her as she tap-danced with excitement around her mother. She couldn't have been more than five or six.

"Excellent choice. I think this hot pink number may be the right size for you." Jack pulled the bright bicycle to the middle of floor. As he hadn't noticed her, Mary quickly stepped back behind the clothes rack. She didn't want to interrupt, but she was entranced by the scene unfolding before her.

He helped little Alison climb onto the bike, holding it steady with his strong tanned arms. "Okay, honey, now rest both feet on the pedals."

She watched Jack work with the girl, reassuring her as he assessed the fit, gently teasing, yet encouraging, too. He checked and rechecked, adjusting the seat height several times until he was satisfied. He seemed so focused, as if nothing was more important than to make this child's first bike exactly right for her. Jack even endured little girl fidgets with a patience Mary never would've believed him capable of, if she hadn't seen it with her own eyes.

Then again, she'd never seen Jack this way before, had she? He was in his own element, doing one of the things he loved best. Here there was no past to live down, no judgments to live up to. Here he could just be.

She felt awash with a tenderness so strong and unexpected that it floored her.

The buoyant excitement about her news collapsed like a punctured tire tube as the ramifications of her feelings sank in. Suddenly the need to tell Jack about her trip to Boston wasn't that compelling. She realized she didn't want to tell him about it at all. In fact, for a flash of an instant she regretted that she had to go.

How could this have happened? She'd been trying, really trying, to keep control of the situation—of herself. This was supposed to be her time, her chance, with no outside considerations hindering her. Certainly she wasn't supposed to be concerned about how her choices would affect Jack. Confused, and feeling more than a little bit threatened, Mary backtracked through the clothing section and slipped out of the store.

She stopped briefly at Twice as Nice to say goodbye and then hurried home to pack. Throwing open a small suitcase on her bed, Mary ignored the blinking red light on the telephone answering machine. It didn't matter who'd called—she was out of here.

She grabbed some underwear from her drawers and stuffed them into shoes. As she picked through her closet, the phone rang again. Letting the machine pick up the call, she turned down the volume. If it was Jack she didn't want to know. If it was Jack she... damn! What was he doing to her? There was a connection between them, a connection that had crept up on her and then whacked her with the force of a ten-ton gorilla.

This was impossible to deal with. She didn't love Jack, she couldn't. It was not in her nature to fall quickly for a man, never mind one she had so many questions about.

Whatever the link between them, it was flimsy at best. Certainly it was nothing to detract her from what she wanted for her life. And heaven knows Jack Candelaria was the last person who could argue with her. She didn't have to call Jack back. Tacking a note on his door upstairs would suffice. She didn't owe him any more than that.

Mary scribbled a brief note, took a quick shower and changed into a comfortable T-shirt and jeans for the long drive to Boston. While her hair air-dried, she placed a suit and two dresses on top of her other things in the suitcase. She was so intent on folding the garments to minimize their wrinkling that she jumped at the knock on her apartment door.

"Mary. Are you still here?" Jack knocked again. "Mary?"

She couldn't believe he'd come. Still here? How did he find out she was leaving?

With a calmness that belied her apprehension, Mary zipped up the suitcase and carried it into the living room. Jack knocked and called out again. Putting the suitcase down, she went to the door.

Relief flashed across his face when she opened it, but then he glanced down at her suitcase. A fierceness darkened his gaze. "Why did you run out of the store?"

"I didn't run out of the store." She closed the door behind him, bullying herself to hold on to her composure. After all, she wasn't even in love with him. "You were busy and I was running out of time."

"Diane told me you had to go to Boston. Why didn't you answer my calls?"

"I've been in such a rush this afternoon," she said, fetching her blue blazer from the hall closet, "I didn't even check the answering machine."

"So you were going away without telling me." Unlike his gaze, his voice was unnervingly calm.

Shrugging on the jacket, Mary got the note she'd written and handed it to him. "I was going to leave you this."

Without even looking at it, Jack crumpled the note in his hand with disgust.

"Have you asked yourself why you're rushing off like this?" he demanded, a seething anger beginning to tinge his words. "Or why you haven't even looked me in the eye since I got here?"

That did it, that was enough for her, and she was almost grateful that he'd pushed her to this point. No longer was she afraid that the emotions unfurling inside of her would spill out in frazzled tears. Resentment gave her strength to fight back.

"I refuse to second-guess myself, Jack. I don't want to lose another chance."

"A chance to what?" he lashed out. "Go live in the great big city all by yourself? I've done that, Mary, and it's vastly overrated."

"You can mock me all you want, but it won't change how I feel. I won't be held back by something—something I'm—"

"Something what, Mary?" Jack took a step toward her, and when she turned to spin away he caught her arm. "Something what?"

She tried to pull free, but his grip was ironclad. She didn't care for this one bit. These emotional dramatics of his scared her—his very intensity threatening to swallow her up, threatening to keep her where he thought she belonged. Finally getting control of her voice, she glared up at him. "I won't be held back by something I'm not sure about. Something that could make me lose out again."

"By something you mean me."

"Of course you'd think that." She gave a rebellious tug, but he held firm.

"You won't even admit it, will you? You have feelings for me that you have to contend with, and you don't like it."

"I certainly don't like having to take you into account any time I want to go out of town for a few days," she snapped.

"Seems to me that's the least of your concerns right now."

He sounded so sure of himself she wanted to smack him. "Look, Jack, I'm not letting you or anyone hold me back this time."

"So instead, you're going to hold yourself back from me." Suddenly all his bluster evaporated, and he looked almost wounded. "Don't you care at all?"

"Yes, I care," she admitted with some reluctance. "But I also have to be realistic."

"Are you being realistic about me?"

"I can't afford not to be. And isn't that the whole point?" Her resolve softening, she tried again to move away.

But he held on. "You're not the only one who stands to lose."

Caught up in the soul-deep expression of his eyes, the fight went out of her. Her knees felt weak. "I know," she whispered.

Apparently sensing her melting resistance, Jack drew her to him. "I want you, Mary. I'm crazy with wanting you. And there's not a damn thing I can do to change that." His hands moved to her shoulders and pulled her closer. "I don't want to change it."

"Even if I bring you nothing but grief?"

"What do you mean *if?*" The corners of his mouth lifted in a wry little smile that had a wallop of an effect on her pulse. "Besides, you're worth the chance— more than worth it. And I kind of hoped you felt that way about me."

"Oh, I do. I may be crazy, but I do."

In resignation and relief she sank into his arms. Her skin felt hot and her heart was thumping wildly. She needed the support of his sturdy strength. His mouth covered hers in a kiss urgent in its hunger, his tongue probing, inciting her to respond, and she did, with all the pent-up longing in her heart. This was inevitable, this was meant to be, and it felt so good.

"Jack," she gasped when he finally released her, but there was no time to come up for air. He kissed the crown of her head and trailed more kisses down the length of her hair, his mouth pausing at her ear to caress it with a moist, torturous sweetness that electrified her entire body.

"Feel how much I need you," he growled, lowering his hands to grip her hard against his hips, "how I want you."

And she wanted him. She pressed even closer, his arousal inflaming a need that licked her loins with searing white heat. Excitement flared within her, like thousands of tiny sparklers sizzling with the desire that would no longer be denied. She lifted her gaze and recognized long-suppressed hunger in his eyes. What fools they'd both been to think they could distance themselves from something this intense.

"I've ached for you," she finally let herself admit, "ached to be with you."

Their eyes locked in mutual expectancy, Jack pushed her blazer off her shoulders and then eased her to the floor. She gave herself up to the kisses, the touches, the sensations, and eventually, to the delight of lying naked in each other's arms. His hands skimmed over her body, arousing with his fingers, tasting with his tongue. But the freedom to take this pleasure from him and, even more, to show her ardor was a potent intensifier. Here and now was what mattered, not what lurked behind the door of tomorrow.

With whispered words and steaming caresses meant to tantalize, Mary revealed her bottled-up desire, expressed her need. She held nothing back. There'd be no more holding back. And the depth and fervor of her passion didn't overwhelm Jack. He accepted it all.

"You want this?" He searched her eyes, and when she nodded, he left her for a moment to reach into his pants pocket. She watched him, gratified that he was prepared to protect her, excited that he wanted her that much.

"Baby, we've wasted so much time," he whispered feverishly when he returned to her, covering her body with his own.

"Much too much," she echoed, pulling him down to kiss him deeply. His groan vibrated in her mouth, and she instinctively arched up, opening body and soul to him.

She was ready... so ready.

A moan of joy escaped her lips when he entered her, and then she was lost as they moved hungrily together. His hands roamed on her breasts to her thighs and back as she rode with the pleasure building inside of her. Her body tightened from head to toe just before an onslaught of incredible sensations rumbled through her. Feeling her climax, he murmured her name over and over until he reached his own shuddering release.

Once the rippling tension finally ceased, Jack opened his eyes. His gaze, smoldering with satisfaction, sought hers. Then he captured her mouth with a long, fierce kiss that she blissfully gave herself up to. She clung to him, feeling womanly, complete.

Jack moved into a spoon position behind her, his arms enveloping her in the moist embrace of afterglow. After the thrilling passion they had shared, it was soothing to just hold each other. Yet the perfection of their lovemaking and the peace of this quiet intimacy was threatened by the twinges of fear creeping up on her. Now that she was coming back down to earth, the reality of their situation was waiting for her: she had to be in Boston by morning, and soon she'd be there for good.

"Mary, where have you drifted off to?" Jack murmured in her ear, his chin nestled on the curve of her shoulder.

"To tomorrow and the next day and the day after that." She sighed deeply. "Oh, Jack, it's hard to take this all in. So much has changed—yet nothing's changed."

His arms quickened around her. "You're not sorry, are you?"

"Absolutely not." She planted a kiss on his arm, drinking in the feel and scent of his damp skin. "I can't regret that. But I'm worried about the door we've just opened, afraid of where it'll lead."

His fingers curved beneath her chin, gently turning her to face him. "It had to happen, you know. We needed to connect this way—it's been building since the moment we met."

"I know." She could see her face reflected in his shimmering brown eyes; she could almost feel their spirits meshing. Yes, they were two of a kind, odd as that would've sounded to her over a month ago. Propelled by the tenderness filling her heart, her hand reached to caress his face. Then she kissed him with all the feeling welling up inside of her.

"Oh, Miss Mary," Jack gasped when she finally released him, "you've got to be one of the all-time great kissers."

"Oh? And are you in a position to rate them?"

He laughed heartily, his naked frame vibrating against her. "Candelaria men don't kiss and tell."

"I'm glad to hear it." She ruffled up his hair, smiling until the old mantel clock in the bedroom chimed five times—another reminder of reality on the march. "Jack, I'm going to have to leave soon."

The light went out of his eyes. "I know. I'll miss you."

"I'll be back in a few days."

"This time."

Not knowing what to say to this, she let her head rest on his chest.

After a few moments Jack sat up to look at her, his expression suddenly brighter. "We've lost track of one basic fact. You're not traveling to the ends of the earth, only Boston."

"That's right." Laughing, she threw her arms around his neck. "That's absolutely right."

He pulled her close, crushing her bare breasts to his smooth, hard chest. "I could come meet you there in a day or two—if you'd like."

"I'd like very much." Like? She was ecstatic.

He grinned, his fingers playing in her hair. "While you're attending to business, I'll have a chance to clear out a few last items from the Lexington house and meet with the attorney. Then, at night, it'll be just you and me."

"Mmm." She closed her eyes, her forehead cradled against his cheek. This was better than anything she could've imagined a few hours ago when she'd been torn and confused. They had made spectacular love and Jack had offered to join her in Boston. Soon she'd have him all to herself, away from the defining confines of Peek Street and Springfield.

It was delicious to think about, and it also gave her hope. There were no guarantees, but perhaps—just perhaps—Jack would want to be part of her future. Spending time together in Boston could only help.

"Mary, you don't have to leave right this minute, do you?" His voice was raspy as his fingers gently taunted her left nipple, rousing an unsettling warmth in her belly. She felt him come alive.

"Depends on what you have in mind." She nuzzled against him.

"Making love in a bed," he growled in her ear, "at least once before you leave."

"Oh, but I have such a long drive ahead of me," she teased, in spite of increasingly shallow breaths.

"And you deserve a proper send-off." He slowly rose to his feet, pulling her up with him.

She gazed into his eyes and found nothing the least bit "proper" in them. "Maybe staying a little longer won't hurt."

"Won't hurt at all." Smiling, Jack lifted her in his arms and carried her into the bedroom.

Jack had not set foot inside his house in the Boston suburbs since the day he'd packed up his car and moved back home to Springfield. He'd hired a cleaning service to dust and vacuum, a lawn service to cut the grass and a security service to install a variety of burglar and fire alarms. Then he'd put the old colonial he'd loved briefly, with a renovator's passion, out of his mind.

Now, after three months, he was back—for the last time. He wasn't thrilled about returning to pack up the pictures and mementos that the real estate agent had insisted he leave out, so the house would have a lived-in look while on the market. But knowing Mary Piletti was waiting for him in the city made this final duty of his old life bearable. He'd plow through the house, get the job done and hurry off to her.

Because he missed her. Lord, how he missed her. Although it'd been only two days since she'd left Springfield—two days since they'd made love—it felt more like two weeks. Which did not bode well for the prospects of a long-distance relationship. He had to deal with that, he knew. And he would... after he'd dealt with this house... after he and Mary had spent more time together.

Carrying cardboard boxes in from the car, Jack started in the living room where the expensive furnishings and period reproductions were dusted and polished and in the same perfect arrangement they'd been in for seven years. This was the first room he and Sandra had decorated. Recalling all the thought and money they'd put into it, he shook his head. They'd never had the time to enjoy the room, or the rest of the house for that matter. With his demanding work hours and Sandra's extensive travel schedule, this beautiful house had become nothing more than a way station: a place to change clothes and grab a night's sleep before heading back out to the jungle.

Jack got to work packing the silver-framed photographs on the grand piano. There weren't many because Sandra's family had requested to have her photographs, following her death. After collecting his college diploma, business awards and racing trophies from the den, he made a quick spot check of the rooms upstairs. Finally the only thing left to do was to grab the good suits he'd left hanging in the cedar closet in the spare bedroom. Then he'd be out of there.

Yet once inside the unfurnished room, he froze. The hollow sound of his steps bounced off the bare floor and walls, and the regret he'd been sidestepping all morning pierced his heart. He swallowed hard. This room, so neglected in comparison with the meticulous decor of the others, was to have had a vital role in the life of this house. He and Sandra had chosen this room to be the nursery—for a new family to replace the one lost to him. Except the room had remained empty to the very end...as empty as their marriage.

Jack slouched against a wall and stared out the window overlooking the wide front lawn. The old oaks and maples were just beginning to turn color, the sky was bright blue and cloudless. What a gift life was, and he was grateful for another chance to get it right. Sandra never got that chance, and it pained him to think of it. She'd deserved better.

"To hell with the suits," he muttered, walking out of the room, shutting the door on the regret it held for him. He had an honest-to-God life to live now with his mother, Peter and the kids, the bike shop, even crazy Peek Street.

And, lucky fool that he was, he had a warm, sweet, gorgeous woman waiting for him at a hotel in town. Mary. He had Mary—he hoped.

The sight of her lifted Jack's heart immediately. She sat alone in the hotel tearoom, unaware that he'd arrived. He approached the table quietly.

"Excuse me, miss, but I couldn't help noticing you sitting here all by yourself," he said. "You're alone?"

She looked up from her teacup. "I am."

"Doesn't seem right for a pretty woman like you to be alone."

"No. It doesn't." Her expression was aloof, her voice cool. But she pushed the vacant chair out from beneath the table with her foot.

He glanced at the chair and then back at her. "May I join you?"

"If you like," she replied, sounding as if she couldn't care less.

With an acknowledging nod, he sat. No sooner had he pulled himself in, than his legs were captured between her ankles. "I thought you'd never get here," she murmured from across the table, nailing him with that sexy gold-green gaze of hers.

"I couldn't get here fast enough." He clasped her hands between his. At last Mary smiled, and Jack felt his spirits soar along with his desire.

"Would you like a cup of tea?"

"Not on your life."

He squeezed her hands, drinking in the message she was sending with her eyes as her shoeless foot caressed his leg underneath the table. She was pushing him to a fast boil. He reached into his jacket pocket for a heavy brass room key, pleased it wasn't one of those plastic cards the big hotel chains handed out these days.

"I happen to have a room here." He put the key down on the table. "Perhaps you'd like to powder your nose."

"Powder my nose?" Her gaze dipped briefly to the key. Then she snapped it up and got to her feet. She bent to whisper in his ear, "Not on your life."

Hand in hand they left the tearoom. But for Jack, the trip from the elegant lobby up to the eighth floor of the classy old hotel tortured his patience. Even in the elevator he and Mary were not alone, thanks to the cheery, uniformed operator. By the time Jack unlocked the door to his suite and pulled her inside, he was on fire.

He swept her into his arms, wanting her like he'd never wanted a woman before. After the morning's cold memories, he had to feel Mary's warmth, needed her vital spirit to fill his lonely soul. Yet he couldn't seem to hold her close enough, couldn't kiss her deep enough, couldn't get her into bed to wrap himself around her soon enough.

"Mary, I need you so," he breathed between kisses.

"Jack, please," she rasped, pulling at his shirt, her urgency matching his. She helped him undress, her soft touch skimming across his bare skin, soothing yet taunting at the same time. Stepping back, she slipped her light summer dress off her shoulders, letting it fall to the floor. He had no words to say how he felt as she stood before him in her lacy white lingerie. There were no words to express what was churning inside him—all he could do was hold his arms out to her.

She walked into his embrace, letting his hands roam the curves and hollows of her silky body before breaking away to lead him into the bedroom. They fell on the thick, quilted bedspread together, and he quickly covered her body with his own, unable to wait any longer.

Mary was there for him, opening herself to him, welcoming his desire, accepting his overwhelming need. How he needed her—all of her—her flesh, her touch, her laughter, her hope, her trust in him. And she gave it all willingly, lovingly, renewing his faith in possibilities and in himself. She cried out his name, clutching him tight as his own release followed, fast and powerful.

When his breathing finally evened out, he sought her eyes. "I missed you."

She rewarded him with a provocative, closed-mouth smile. Then she answered, "I can tell."

"If someone said to me—say three months ago— that I'd be making mad, passionate love to little Mary Piletti in a hotel room, I'd have said they were stark raving bonkers."

She chuckled. "I would've said worse."

Gentle teasing and languid kisses settled them down after their tumultuous encounter, and when Mary excused herself from the bed, he reluctantly let her go. Soon he heard water running.

"Jack, come see what I've found," she called from the bathroom.

In the sizable and luxurious bathroom, Mary stood at the foot of a huge whirlpool bath, rapidly filling with water. She held out her hand. "Care to join me?"

They sank down into the hot swirling water together, side by side, legs and arms entwined. Jack lay back, content after making love and so relaxed as the water steamed through his pores. He'd be happy to soak there with Mary for hours and then make love again and again. And since they'd planned to spend the entire next day together, maybe they'd do just that.

Beside him, Mary sighed. "So far, this is undeniably the best day of my life."

"That good, huh?"

"Perfect would not be an exaggeration."

"I take it things are going well with the Michael sisters." Selfish of him as it was, the last thing he wanted to discuss right now was Mary's business doings. Yet her eyes had brightened when he'd mentioned it. He couldn't deny her the pleasure of talking about it.

"Jack, this thing is really going to fly. The Brook-line location is prime. Lorna and Terry and I agree on most of the major points. And it's possible we could be up and running by the first of the year."

As he listened to her talk about timetables, inventories, additional locations, he heard her eagerness. He also felt her slipping away from him. He tried to fight the feeling, telling himself he was being too possessive, that he shouldn't overreact. But his attempts were undermined by the look in her eyes, a look he knew all too well. He'd seen it in Sandra each time she'd landed a hot new account or job promotion. And each time she would swear they'd start a baby soon. Soon.

Of course, he had to share in the blame. Back then he'd been just as gung ho about his career. He'd put in his share of eighteen-hour days, taking advantage of the opportunities that had come his way—and some that hadn't. So how could he fault Mary for jumping at a great opportunity and being thrilled about it?

He couldn't.

But he resented it like hell.

Chapter Ten

The expression on Jack's face stopped her cold.

"Jack, are you all right?" she asked, realizing she'd been babbling on. "Jack?"

Her question pulled his attention back and he shrugged, making the bath water ripple across their bodies. "Guess I got distracted."

She stroked his arm beneath the water. "I'm sorry, I didn't even ask you how things went at the house. Was it difficult?"

"No more than one would expect."

His flat, unrevealing answer was oh-so-typical; she wanted to shake him. Hard.

She was painfully aware that, since returning to Springfield, Jack had said little about his late wife and his marriage. Why? Was he still grieving for Sandra, despite what was now developing between the two of them? It was possible. Yet she had a nagging feeling there was something else, something that made him uncomfortably chary whenever the topic of his marriage came up.

"Tell me about this morning, Jack."

He shook his head. "It's part of the past, Mary."

"It's part of you." She cupped his face between her hands, urging him with her eyes. "We need to talk about this."

He sank a little deeper into the tub. "Going back was difficult. Much harder than I thought it would be."

"Oh, Jack, I'm sorry."

"It was hard, but not for the reasons you'd expect. Good memories had nothing to do with it," he said, sounding almost angry. "Being back in that house just reminded me of empty, wasted years—years I can never have back."

"I don't understand."

He looked away from her and stared down at the bubbling water. "Sandra and I were legally separated when she was killed in the accident. In fact, we were in the middle of a divorce."

"A divorce?"

"No one in Springfield knows about it. I never told my family. There didn't seem to be any reason to."

She was stunned. All she could do was stare at him.

"We grew apart—or stopped growing—or didn't have the time to grow. Sure we looked like we had it all—fantastic jobs, great house, expensive cars, plenty of money. What we didn't have was time for each other and our marriage. We were both so busy working to build our careers and maintain our life-style, we

ended up with nothing. Don't you see, Mary," he im-
plored, "I couldn't live like that anymore."

"You wanted the divorce?"

"I asked for it, though Sandra agreed it was for the
best. Her career was taking off, and she wanted to focus on it exclusively. But I wanted more . . . I wanted a
life."

"A life in Springfield," she said softly. Things were
beginning to fall into place now.

"It took me a little longer to figure that out. Only
after I'd decided to get off the fast track did I realize
how shallow my life had become." He reached for her
hand and held it tight. "The whole skeleton of my existence crumbled. I had no real friends, only business
associates. I hardly knew my neighbors, and it didn't
matter, anyway, because I knew I had to sell the house
as part of the divorce settlement." Jack looked at her.
"What a great life I managed to make for myself,
right?"

She didn't know how to answer, and he didn't wait
for one. "Then Sandra died, and—" He paused, taking a deep breath. "And all those years we wasted have
been haunting me ever since. Instead of staying and
making things work, I walked away—just like I
walked away from my father and Peek Street."

Mary felt the tension in his body, saw the sadness in
his eyes, and her heart ached for him. She squeezed his
hand. "So you came home."

"Home," he repeated, shaking his head. "When we
were kids, my mother told Peter and me that family
was forever. People would come and go, but we'd always have each other. But the last twenty years had me
convinced otherwise—until the day I realized I had

nothing, absolutely nothing. That's when I knew I wanted to come back."

"To a less-than-enthusiastic welcome."

"But not unexpected. I didn't, however, expect to find you." He lifted her hand from the tub and pressed it to his lips.

Mary had never fully realized what Jack's return to Springfield meant to him, nor what he'd gone through to get there. The picture was clearer now. By going home, Jack had made a serious, deeply personal life choice—an understandable one. Still, there were questions.

"Has finding me made any difference?"

"For the present I'd say it makes all the difference." Then his gaze darkened. "As for the future? You tell me, Mary."

Tell him? Suddenly that wasn't so easy. Enthralled by their new intimacy, she'd hoped—half hoped—that he would want to join her here in a new life. Given what he'd told her, she couldn't just blurt that out. Yet maybe she could make him understand.

"Perhaps with a different set of goals," she began, nervously, "and with a different type of woman, it wouldn't—"

"Don't, Mary, please. If you think I'd move back here, you're wrong. I don't have the heart for it. This morning at the house convinced me all over again," he insisted. "Besides, things would be different between us here—we'd be different. I don't want that to happen."

"What about what I want?"

He took a long time to answer, and although he didn't move, she could feel him pulling away. Even his brown-eyed gaze seemed distant. "Let's face it, Mary, I *am* selfish, just like they've been saying on Peek Street for years. If you didn't believe it before, now you have proof."

Dragging himself out of the tub, he grabbed a thick white towel off the rack and wrapped it around his trim waist. "I'm sorry to be so direct," he said, crouching down beside the tub. "But mincing words isn't going to help anything."

"I know." She swallowed hard, unable to meet his eyes.

"Look, we'll talk more about this at dinner." He gently brushed a damp strand of hair from her cheek. "I'm going to get dressed now."

Alone, Mary sank deeper into the water, knowing Jack was being nothing but truthful. He'd recognized what he wanted for his life and he'd come home to get it. He certainly wasn't about to step backward, not even for her. He was selfish. Strong-headed and determined, too. But he was also compassionate, fun, sexy, adventurous, tender. And, God help her, she was in love with him.

She couldn't hide from it.

Engrossing as her meetings with the Michael sisters had been, Jack had never left her thoughts. She'd been literally counting the hours before their scheduled rendezvous in the hotel tearoom. She didn't want him to be that important to her, but he was. She loved him, and it was too late to do anything about it. Yet what hope was there for this love if it was already calling for sacrifice—her sacrifice?

Jack knocked on the door and brought in her suitcase, which the concierge had just delivered to the suite. When he left, Mary toweled off and dressed with care, if not enthusiasm. She'd been so excited yesterday when she'd bought the formfitting little black dress for this evening's night on the town. She had hoped Jack would love it, but now it scarcely mattered.

As Mary made her way from the bathroom to the suite's living room, she heard the telephone ring.

"It's for you," Jack said when she entered the room. "Lorna Michael."

She had told Lorna she was moving to this hotel tonight—in case anything needing immediate attention came up. But the aloof look on Jack's face when he handed her the phone made her wish she hadn't. She turned away from him, listening to what Lorna had to say, yet intensely aware of Jack's eyes on her back. The call was brief.

"They want me to stay in town an extra day or two," Mary announced when she hung up. "They've just learned of an alternative location in Brookline that we should take a look at in the morning—in case the first one falls through. And the attorney wants to sit down with the three of us again to iron out a few more details."

Jack sat down on the cranberry red sofa. "We have plans to spend the day together. Remember?"

"I haven't forgotten. But I have to do this." She joined him on the couch. "It shouldn't take more than a few hours. That leaves us the afternoon. Or maybe you can stay an extra day?"

"My shop's been open only a couple of months. I can't take that much time away from it. Not yet."

"And I can't tell Lorna and Terry that I'm not coming," she said, struggling with a rising resentment. "So what would you have me do, Jack?"

"You don't want to know."

"Maybe you ought to say it, anyway."

"Fine." He got to his feet and began pacing in front of her. "I want to sleep with you in my arms all night and make love to you all morning. Then, if and when we get out of bed, I want us to roam around town as we'd planned. And, yes, I want you to come back to Springfield with me tomorrow night."

There it was again—what *he* wanted.

"Jack, all that would be wonderful, but now something has come up, and I have to tend to it."

"You can dig yourself into a hole with *have-to*s, Mary. Believe me, I know. We choose to do what we do, and you have every right to choose for yourself."

"You mean I can choose what you want or choose what I need to do." She was tired of living according to what other people wanted or needed—she had wants and needs of her own. "You've had some rough times, Jack. I can see how what happened in your marriage can make you wary of—of what I want. But you've got to understand that I can't live my life making up for where yours went wrong."

His gaze flinched, making her feel like she'd slapped him. He stopped his slow pacing and stared down at her on the sofa. "Like I said, it's your choice."

"Yes, it is." She loved him, but now she had little hope for it. As much as it pained her, she was beginning to believe this wasn't the kind of love that could endure giving up her dream again. Because that would be like giving up on herself. "My choice is to meet with

Lorna and Terry tomorrow, stay the extra couple of days or as long as necessary."

"I see. Well, you know what's best for you."

She couldn't read his eyes, yet she prayed he'd consider her side of the situation. "We still have tonight, Jack, and we can have tomorrow afternoon."

But he shook his head. "I can't do it, Mary. It'd just be prolonging the inevitable, and I'm too old to play that game."

"How can you be so damn sure what'll happen? You can't possibly know."

"Look at us now," he said, holding his arms out wide in frustration. "We've been together in Boston for exactly three hours, and already we're at each other's throats."

"That's because you're being downright stubborn."

"I don't deny it, and I won't apologize for it, either." He reached down to caress her cheek. "I think I'd better go."

His tender touch almost drove her to tears, but his words steeled her against them. "You're leaving now?"

"It sounds like you have a big day ahead of you tomorrow, and I have a long drive home tonight."

There didn't seem much left to say after that. He was walking out. Feeling numb inside, she watched Jack gather his belongings. He pulled on a dark blue suit jacket, and Mary realized this was the first time she'd seen him dressed up in a proper suit. He looked devastatingly handsome. Of course, amid the turmoil, he hadn't noticed her new black dress, which she had bought with him—and tonight—in mind.

Soon after Jack had left the suite, Mary could hear the chime of the old-fashioned elevator outside in the hall as it arrived on the floor to take him away. The heavy clank of the door shutting behind him was the loneliest sound she'd ever heard. Finally the tears she'd coolly held on to in Jack's presence now streamed down her face, unbidden and unrestrained.

Jack returned to Springfield hell-bent on getting his life on track. No more detours. On his first day back he got Mario Piletti cracking on finding some new house listings, he officially made Leo the assistant manager of the shop and then he put his brother at the top of his list of priorities.

He also tried to think of Mary as little as possible.

Yet he kept picturing her sitting in the suite, a knockout in that sexy black dress, glaring up at him with both anger and confusion. At one point she'd looked like she might break into tears, although it was tough for him to imagine Mary actually crying. She was the most resilient woman he'd ever known, nurturing, compassionate, and—unfortunately for him—extremely determined. . . .

So much for not thinking about Mary Piletti!

She had made her choice and there wasn't a damn thing he could do about it. The irony of the whole thing was he had thought he could handle whatever happened between them. But hell, walking out of that hotel suite was no piece of cake. He hadn't wanted to leave, except he could only foresee trouble and heartache down the road if he'd stayed. After all, he possessed a certain track record in that regard. Mary deserved better. Much better.

And his life had to go on.

Turning his attention to Peter, Jack was impatient to sit him down to talk about the future. But his brother managed to cross him up at every turn. Peter conveniently missed a family dinner, forgot a lunch meeting Jack had talked him into and blatantly avoided Jack's telephone calls. Instead of putting him off, however, Peter's stunts made Jack more determined than ever. The two of them had already lost twenty years—Jack couldn't abide wasting more precious time. Once Peter knew what Jack wanted to do for him, he was sure it would make all the difference.

Passing by his mother's house on his way to work one morning, Jack spotted Peter's car still in the driveway. "It's now or never," he muttered, as he took a sharp left into the drive, pulling up right behind the gray sedan. With his car blocking Peter's, there was no way his kid brother could leave until he was good and ready to let him.

As he walked around to the back door, he noticed Gina's car was gone. If he was lucky, Peter would be home alone. Jack took a deep breath and let himself in, trying to act as if dropping by to see his brother was the most natural thing in the world.

He found Peter sitting at the kitchen table reading the morning paper.

"Hey, brother, you're just the man I want to see," he said casually, grabbing a clean mug from a cabinet and pouring himself some coffee. "You alone?"

Peter stiffened when Jack sat down at the table. "Gina took the kids to school. Ma's with her. I think they're stopping at the grocery store on the way back."

Then he glanced at his watch. "And I've got to be running along because Charlie—"

"I've been wanting to talk to you for weeks." Jack stopped Peter with a firm hand on his arm. "Hear me out, Pete."

Grimacing, Peter sat back down. "Make it quick."

"Okay, I'll dispense with the niceties. Look, I've got some money to invest, and I've heard you're pretty good at selling real estate. Top-notch as a matter of fact. I thought you might be interested in going into business together—with me strictly being a silent partner, that is." He paused to gauge his brother's reaction, but Peter's face was blank. "What do ya say? Interested?"

Peter looked him right in the eye. "Not at all."

"What?"

"I'm not interested."

"I'm offering you a chance to own your own business, be your own boss, run your own show. How can you not be interested?"

"Easy. I don't want to work for you."

"Not *for* me. We'd be partners."

Peter stood up from the table, his gaze full of resentment. "Don't give me that, Jack. If it's your money, it's your business. And you'll be the hero, the wonderful guy who's taking care of little brother by throwing his money around. Hey, what a great way to show what a rich success you've become."

Stunned, Jack got to his feet at once. "That's not it at all. I'm offering you a chance to start over."

"Who the heck are you to come back and give second chances?" Peter's face reddened as his voice grew more agitated. "Is it to make you feel better for skipping out on us all those years ago? Everything went to hell in a hand basket because you left. So now that Dad's long gone, you finally get up the nerve to come back, thinking you can set it all right again?"

Peter's barbs cut him to the quick, but Jack was determined to stay calm. "I'd like to think it's a chance for you and me to mend fences. And yes, maybe it's a way to help pay back for how I let you down. But I've returned to Springfield to start over, and I want to give you the opportunity to start over, too."

"Start over? I'm not twenty years old anymore," Peter scoffed. "I can't go jumping into some cockamamy scheme designed to alleviate your guilt or buck you up because you couldn't hack it out in the real world and had to run home to 'start over.' Unlike you, I've got responsibilities. Like a wife and three kids—and Ma."

"I'll help with Ma from here on in," Jack said tightly, his temper strained to the limit. "If you'd just settle down and forget the past for a moment, you'd see that this is something you really should do. You tell me what you need, it's yours—I'll stay out of it."

"I don't need you, Jack. I've got a job."

"You're dreaming if you think you can work at Piletti's for the rest of your life. Besides, you shouldn't want to." He ran his hand through his hair in frustration. Why was it so difficult to talk sense into this guy? "Look, I'm telling you, an opportunity like this may never come your way again. You should take it."

Peter gave him a snide glare. "Right hotshot, I should do it because you say so."

A heavy thud sounded from behind them. They both turned to find Gina had dropped a heavy bag of groceries on the kitchen counter. Rose stood right behind her with the baby in her arms.

Gina looked livid. "Maybe you should do it because it's the best thing to happen to you in fifteen years."

"How long have you been standing there?" Peter asked, shaken.

"Long enough to hear what Jack's offering you." She threw her purse on the kitchen table. "And long enough to see you throw it away. How could you, Peter? You're absolutely miserable at work. You've wanted your own business for years."

"That's right—my own business. Not Jack's. I'm not taking anything from him."

"So you'd rather stay unhappy and bitter, making everybody around you miserable," Gina flared. "Well, I'm sick and tired of it."

Jack stood there, stunned, desperate to figure out some way to cool things down. He glanced over at his mother, still standing in the doorway with little Elizabeth. Perhaps guessing at what was on his mind, she shook her head at him. Of course, she was right. What could he say that would smooth things over now?

"Does acting like a martyr make you feel important, Peter?" cried Gina. "I think it does. Blaming someone else is so much easier than—"

"Stop it, Gina. Don't say another word."

"I've kept quiet too long, while you blamed Jack and your father and even poor Rose for your own failings." Tears flowing down her cheeks, Gina looked sadly at Rose before turning back to Peter. "And do you know why I did? Because I was terrified that you'd blame me and the kids next."

"Gina, I never..." Peter rushed to her side but she pulled away.

"But I don't care anymore," she continued between sobs. "Jack coming back is not a horrible thing. His offer to help you is not a horrible thing. And if you refuse to see that, if you can't swallow your pride and do something not only for your family, but for yourself, then I can't—I—I won't live this way anymore."

Gina rushed out of the kitchen and up the stairs. Instead of going after her, Peter turned on Jack with eyes blazing with anger. "Are you satisfied now? Think you've done enough damage? Or should we wait to see what else you can destroy while you're at it?"

"I never meant for anything like this to happen."

"You never meant," Peter mimicked with disdain as he reached for the suit jacket hanging on the back of a kitchen chair. "Well, I'll tell you something I mean with all my heart—I wish to hell you had never come back."

"Peter, wait," he called as Peter hurried out the back door, brushing past Rose.

Jack started to follow, but Rose stopped him. "Let him go."

"But I've got to talk some sense into him," he protested, watching Peter hop into Gina's station wagon.

"No!" She grabbed his arm with her free hand as the baby squirmed. Her adamance drew his gaze. He'd never seen her like this: her face ashen with sorrow, her brown eyes watery with unshed tears. "You've done enough already."

But Jake just sat there some nights. He lost the desire to wish for the hunger. He settled again firmly but pushed his arm with its tick marks on its calendar remorse, and made another one more than before. It would take a gentleness because he was not happy with himself in the way that tomorrow would be more complicated.

Chapter Eleven

Mary felt ambivalent about returning to Springfield. In a span of a week, much in her life had changed. Her partnership with the Michael sisters was practically a done deal—the lawyers had only to draw up the papers. And she and Jack had become lovers—for a few days anyway. Now she didn't know what they were, and this disturbed her more than anything had before. It hurt. But it was her own fault for ignoring her instincts. Wrong man, wrong time . . . why hadn't she listened?

Well, she was paying the price now. As hard as she tried to fight it, she missed Jack—missed him more because she knew they could no longer be close. No more long talks, no more laughing, no more lovemaking. The lines had been drawn, and Mary knew he'd stick as firmly to his side as she would to hers.

Not wanting to face a possible encounter with Jack the minute she got back into town, she bypassed the apartment building and stopped by to see her parents. She found her mother in the kitchen, washing the supper dishes.

Josephine greeted her with a hearty hug. "Your father just left for a parish meeting, he'll be disappointed he missed you." After pouring two cups of coffee, she sat at the kitchen table with Mary. "Now tell me everything that happened in Boston. Are you happy about it? Will these Michael sisters be fair to you?"

"Mother, don't worry. Lorna and Terry are as nice as they can be." She went on to explain about visiting the store sites and other details she thought her mother might enjoy—except for Jack's oh-so-brief visit. There was no need to get her all worked up about that.

"So, it looks like you'll be going to Boston for real. And Diane will manage Twice as Nice for you here?"

"She's done a great job while I've been away, hasn't she? With your help, that is."

"We've managed okay." Josephine shrugged. "Now how soon will this thing be finalized?"

"If all goes well, within a month or two."

"That soon? My, my."

"Which reminds me, I've got to talk to Dad about finding someone else to manage the building. I think Lou Ponzini might be interested."

Josephine frowned as Mary sipped her coffee. "Do you have any idea where you're going to live?"

"Not exactly. Although I checked out a few apartments while I was there."

"Already you've looked into places?"

Mary caught the wariness in her mother's voice and guessed it was understandable. After thirty years her "little girl" was finally leaving the nest.

They sat in silence for a minute or two while Josephine eyed her with curiosity.

"Something else on your mind, Mother?"

"On my mind? No, no." Josephine shook her head. "Well, except...Rose Candelaria mentioned that Jack was in Boston earlier this week."

She should've known. One thing she would not miss was Peek Street's supercharged grapevine. "He was."

"Oh?" Her mother perked up considerably. "Then you saw him?"

"Just briefly. For tea," she added quickly, hoping she didn't sound like she was hiding something. Though she was certain her mother didn't really want to know about the lovemaking in the hotel suite. "I believe he came back to Springfield that same night."

"He should've stayed longer."

"Huh?"

"He would've been better off if he had. Everyone would have."

She didn't like the sound of this. "What do you mean? Has something happened to Jack?"

"Something happened all right," her mother replied, again shaking her head. "All hell has broken loose with the Candelarias, and as usual, Jack's at the center of it."

"Oh, Mom, no! What happened?"

"Rose showed up here last night, sobbing about a huge blowup the two boys had yesterday, and that Gina left with the kids."

"Gina left? But why?"

"Something about a business Jack wanted to start with Peter. Peter wanted nothing to do with it, and they argued," Josephine explained. "I guess Gina wanted Peter to do it, and that started a whole other argument. In the end, Gina took the kids to her mother in New Hampshire and Peter blames Jack for all of it. And, of course, Rose is caught smack in the middle."

"Oh, no, this is awful."

All Mary could think of was how much Jack wanted to mend the rift with his brother. He'd been so excited about giving Peter the chance to own a business—excited and impatient. Now it had backfired in his face.

"It's typical Candelaria dramatics, you know," her mother said. "Those boys get it from their father. Everything is a crisis. Nothing's easy, no one is reasonable. It's a wonder Rose's hair hasn't turned white by now. Candelaria dramatics, that's all this is."

Mary remembered telling herself she'd no intention of getting dragged into the temperamental antics of that family. She, Miss Cool, was going to keep her distance. Still, here she was, sucked well and truly into their emotional cyclone. The Candelarias were in trouble, and she cared very much. She felt badly for Rose, sorry for Gina, and she wanted to give Peter a good kick in the rear. But most of all she was concerned about Jack. She understood that restoring his relationship with Peter was the integral piece to rebuilding his life here. It had meant everything to Jack and now... now he must be devastated. And alone.

"Mom, I've got to go."

"Go?" Josephine looked startled when Mary bolted from the table. "But you haven't even finished your coffee."

Not stopping to respond, Mary hurried to her car and drove off to find Jack. She swung past the bike shop, but it was closed up tight. Then she headed for the apartment building, praying she'd find him home. By the time she ran up the three flights of stairs and knocked on his door, she was breathing hard. Losing patience after several seconds, she knocked again.

Jack answered the door, his brows arched in surprise. "I would say you're the last person I'd expect to find at my door, except I don't expect anybody to come calling these days. When did you get back?"

"About half an hour ago."

"And now you're here? Frankly, Mary, I thought we'd said everything we had to say to each other."

She'd never seen him like this. His vibrance was gone. He looked tired and maybe a little depressed. And his eyes, usually lively and rich with enthusiasm, seemed cautious.

"Look, I heard about what happened between you and Peter."

"And you've been in town all of thirty minutes? God, I love this place."

"Won't you let me in? I thought you might want to talk about it."

"Come in if you want," he said, pushing the door open wide. "But why would I want to talk about how I've managed to tear my family apart—again?"

The cynicism tinging his words troubled her. It wasn't like him. She stepped inside the apartment, which was dark save for the light of one table lamp.

The pillows on the beige sofa were bunched up, the cushions in disarray, and a few empty beer cans and a couple of half-full take-out containers were scattered across the coffee table. The thought of Jack sitting alone in the semidarkness, drinking and barely eating made her heart sink.

After straightening a cushion, she sat on the sofa. "I know you, Jack. I think you need to talk about it."

"Save the pity for somebody else, Mary," he said, staring down at her. "Besides, you don't know me half as well as you think. Wasn't that what our abbreviated visit in Boston was all about?"

She sighed. "Save the self-pity, Candelaria, and sit down. Because, like it or not, I'm the only friend you have in this town. And I'm certainly the only one who cares that there are two sides to the story."

"Mary, I knew from day one you were going to be a royal pain." He plopped himself down beside her.

"Thank you, Jack," she replied with feigned sweetness. "My thoughts about you run along the same vein."

"And the good folk of Peek Street still think that way today."

She looked at him with all seriousness. "Do you care what they think?"

"No. But my family—I've really made a mess of things for them. I'm sick about it."

She touched his shoulder. "Tell me, Jack."

Listening as Jack reluctantly explained what had happened the day before, Mary sensed that sheer impatience caused him to come on a tad too strong for his oversensitive brother. Yet this didn't warrant Jack second-guessing himself.

"You sound like you're questioning why you came back," she told him. "But that's the one thing on which you've been very clear and focused. No one knows that better than me."

"Yeah, the old 'I needed to return to my roots' song and dance. Coming back to what really matters, right?" he said rather belligerently. "Why didn't you tell me to stuff a sock in it, Mary?"

"Because it didn't sound like a song and dance to me! You meant every word you said." She didn't want to lecture him, but she couldn't stand hearing him be this negative.

Jack sat up and met her gaze. "I thought I meant it. But maybe, just maybe, it was a case of running home to hide because I'd messed up my life out there in the real world."

"Oh no, that's your brother talking, and I'm not buying it," she retorted. "From where I sit, it takes no small amount of courage to change direction at your age. You had the smarts to reassess your life, and you saw what was lacking and decided to do something about it. And coming back to Peek Street was far from an easy out."

Jack seemed taken aback. "You really believe that, Mary? Even now?"

"Absolutely. And I'm no pushover."

"Nobody knows that better than me," he admitted, with a wistful sliver of a smile. "Though I was kind of wishing you were a pushover when I was driving home from Boston the other night."

Suddenly she felt awkward. "Jack...I..."

He took her hand, enfolding it between his. "Now I know I wouldn't want you to be anything but what you are. You're special, Mary, and so dear to me."

All sorts of emotions tore through her. Her heart was beating faster now, as her entire being quickened with a familiar excitement. The look in Jack's chocolate eyes melted any resistance she'd built against him over the last several days. Still, she feared that heartbreak was shadowing them, and she should put a stop to the possibility right now. But she couldn't. She felt like throwing up her hands in despair. Being with him was impossible! And it was impossible not to respond to him.

"Coming here the way you did—to support me—means more than I can say." He shook his head as if he couldn't quite believe it. "I'm not sure I deserve—"

"Don't." She pressed her fingers to his lips. "I had to come to you, and I know you'd be there for me if the tables were turned." She believed this with all her heart.

Eyes brimming with unspoken emotion, Jack pulled her into his arms. "Oh, baby," he breathed against her cheek, "I can't tell you how many times I wanted to pick up that phone and call you since this all happened."

"I'm here for you now, Jack," she whispered, touching his cheek. He covered her hand with his own before drawing her close against his chest, holding her as if he would never let her go.

"I thought we wouldn't be together this way again," he murmured in her ear. "I kept telling myself I could handle it, but it was tearing me apart."

The wild pounding of his heart, which she could feel against her breasts, shot ripples of yearning through her body. She hadn't come to him for that, but she realized her reaction was inevitable. Her feelings for him, emotional and physical, were all bound up together. How could she be with Jack and not want him?

Accepting this, she sought his lips, and he answered with an exquisite, deep kiss that fanned her desire.

"Mary, stay with me tonight," he rasped, when he finally came up for air. "I need you."

She was breathless from the longing pumping through her blood—the longing to express her love and desire for him in his arms. "I'll stay," she whispered.

Jack stood up from the sofa and held out his hand. Her entire being focused on his warm gaze, Mary put her hand in his and followed, wordlessly, as he led the way into the bedroom. In the silent dark, she went into his arms without hesitation, needing his enclosing embrace. But even more, she needed to show him how deeply she cared. As they slowly undressed each other with arousing caresses and lingering kisses, her passion flowed with a freedom she'd never experienced before.

Drawing him down onto the bed, she curved herself against his smooth, hard body. She wanted to give everything to him. Every kiss, every touch, every murmur was given to show he wasn't alone. No matter what might happen between them later, she meant to be there for him now. And Jack accepted her gifts with a burning tenderness that made her senses reel. They moved together with increasing fervor until the giving and receiving lifted her to a soul-stirring climax and she cried out her pleasure.

Afterward Jack held her close, and she reveled in how it felt to be in his arms, her skin still tingling from their lovemaking. This time had been different from the others—no less spectacular, but in a way more wonderful. This time their bodies had communicated a passion that carried them beyond the excitement and intriguing newness of desire. Jack must have experienced this, too—she felt it in the way he held her.

At last Jack broke the silence. "How did you know I needed you?" he said, his voice low. "I wouldn't even admit it to myself."

"Don't you know?" Turning to him, she lifted her head above his. "Don't you know I love you?"

He said her name softly as his hands cupped her face. Though after that, he seemed at a loss for words. She looked into his eyes, but in the dark they were impossible to read. Then he drew her face down to him and kissed her deeply until the heat within her stirred anew. For now, this was the only response that mattered as they began to make love again.

He held her closer and tighter than ever before, until she moaned her need for him.

"Don't love me, Mary. Don't love me," he murmured over and over in her ear as he moved inside her. "Don't love me, please. It won't change me."

Mary felt a warm ribbon of heat play across her closed eyes. Only half-awake, she stretched lazily, preparing to burrow deeper under the covers. But the unfamiliar feel of the mattress pricked her eyes open. The sunlight streaming through the cracks of the miniblinds made her blink uncomfortably until she turned to face the other side of the bed—Jack's bed.

Except Jack wasn't there.

Pulling the top sheet over her breasts, she sat up. "Jack?" She called out twice more, but received no reply. When she spotted a robe hanging from a peg inside an opened closet door, she got out of bed and put it on. Then she checked the bathroom, living room, kitchen. No Jack, no note, nothing. Suddenly she felt chilled, and Jack's robe did little to warm her.

He shouldn't have left her like this, not after what had happened between them last night. True, he'd told her not to love him, but the way he'd held her before she fell asleep belied those words. She'd felt loved last night. But in the cold light of morning, what did that mean? When the words she wanted to hear weren't said and the wrong ones were, what did any of it mean?

Mary looked around the living room with its messy debris. She'd come running to Jack's side because he'd needed her. She'd even told him she loved him! He took it all, too: her support, her love, her body. While in his arms, she had even harbored the hope that Jack would want to reconsider their situation and work out a compromise. In return, however, he left her alone and miserable with "Don't love me" ringing in her ears. Well, Jack had admitted he was selfish, and last night he'd told her another hard cold truth—loving him won't change him.

She was bewildered, resentful, hurt. But she didn't know which pained her more—Jack letting her down, or that she'd been a fool for love again.

She marched back into the bedroom to hunt up her clothes. It was after nine and she had to get to the store and tend to her business. There was a lot to take care of in the coming weeks. She couldn't afford to sacrifice her time and energy on futile distractions any longer.

When she arrived at the store forty-five minutes later, her sister-in-law was already there preparing to open up. "Finally the boss is back." Diane, petite and perfectly groomed as usual, greeted her with a hug. "Now we'll get some order around here."

"Ha! You and my mother have been doing just fine without me. In fact, you two don't need me around here anymore." Actually she was grateful for Diane's interest in the store—which she planned to make legal—because it made the transition to Boston much simpler.

"I wouldn't go that far," Diane said as she poured Mary some coffee. "I could never run this place as well as you."

"Oh, sure." Mary sat down at her desk. "I saw those two almost-spanking-new Lady Emily dresses on display out front. How ever did you get your hands on them?"

"Mary, this woman just walked in with bags of the most unbelievable clothes. She dresses her two daughters like little princesses—everything top of the line." Diane leaned lazily against the wall and sighed. "I'd snap up those dresses in a second for my girls except they'd never put up with the froufrou. Sometimes I wish they weren't such tomboys."

"You must have girls I don't know about, because my nieces are perfect," Mary countered with a smile. "It runs in the family."

"Ah, you may want to revise that comment after I tell you what your 'perfect' brother did last night." Diane nervously pushed some blond strands away from her face. "I don't think you'll like it, but I'm afraid Josephine's going to come in here later and give you an earful."

She was mystified. "What is this about?"

Diane sat in the straight-back chair next to the desk. "According to your mother, you ran out of her house like a bat out of hell last night. Is that right?"

"Well, something like that."

"Enough like that to worry her, apparently. Because she called Charlie just as he and I were leaving to go to a movie. She was in such a tizzy, he agreed to stop by your apartment on our way to check on you."

Uneasy, Mary shifted in her chair. "And you didn't find me home."

"No, we didn't. But your car was in the parking lot, so Charlie decided to go upstairs to Jack's—only because he'd found you there once before," Diane added hastily. "Remember?"

"Oh, yes." How could she forget that night?

"So we went up to Jack's and—I'm embarrassed to admit—we listened at the door. We heard your voice and—"

"Why didn't you knock and let us know you were out there?"

"It was all I could do to keep Charlie from barging in," Diane revealed. "But I honestly didn't think you wanted us to, because it sounded like you two were having a pretty intense discussion.''

Mary gave a weary sigh. "Yeah, we were. And I appreciate not being interrupted.''

"Good. But there's more, unfortunately.''

"Unfortunately?''

"You know your brother—he gets overprotective sometimes, and he's a worrier like your mother. As soon as we got back from the movie, he started calling your apartment but kept getting the answering machine. He even tried to call you several times this morning,'' she added, with a trace of awkwardness. "Since we know you never turn off the ring because tenants have to be able to reach you in an emergency, well we... you know.''

"Figured I was still with Jack.'' She felt her face burn.

"Yep. Which is fine because Charlie's no prude—in fact he's kind of tickled about it. In fact, he's dead-certain you and Jack are engaged.''

"What?''

"Well—the thought had occurred to me, too,'' Diane admitted with a sheepish grin. "Maybe because we know Jack went to Boston while you were there. Maybe because we hate the idea of you moving away. Besides, if you're sleeping with him, it really doesn't seem that farfetched.''

Mortified, Mary raked her fingers through her hair, shaking her head. "Well, I'm not sleeping with Jack—not anymore. Things aren't working out. And we're not engaged.''

"I kind of guessed that by the way you looked when you walked in this morning. Not glowing bride-to-be material at all—although I'd hoped I was mistaken."

"You've got to tell Charlie right away," Mary insisted. "I don't want him saying anything to the parents. You don't think he has, do you?"

"I'd better go call him." Diane rose from the chair, but stopped before picking up the phone. "What about Jack?"

She knew what her sister-in-law was asking. "We want different things, Diane."

"Do you? Forgive me for being blunt, Mary, but you're not getting any younger," she warned. "I know you want a family—I've seen how you are with the kids. And I've heard that's why Jack came back to Springfield. Besides, a good man doesn't come around every day, you know."

"Since when has anyone around here considered Jack 'good'?"

"If you care for him—and I believe you do—then he must be."

"You're presuming too much about me and Jack," she said as calmly as she could, realizing her sister-in-law meant well. "As for getting married and having a family, I've got plenty of time."

"I suppose you're right," Diane agreed with a shrug. "Just remember time can get away from you. Don't take it too much for granted."

Jack walked into Twice as Nice, and a sweet, lullaby-sounding chime over the door announced his arrival. As if he wasn't on edge enough already, the crooning chime increased the bull-in-a-china-shop awkwardness he always experienced in Mary's store. With the racks of small-size clothes, the baby stuff, the young mothers shopping and little kids bopping about, he felt out of place and conspicuous.

This afternoon he felt doubly ill at ease because he wasn't anticipating a warm welcome from the proprietor. Nor did he deserve one, not after last night. He'd taken way too much from Mary and had given her so little in return. Not that he didn't want to shower her with the immense feelings he held in his heart. But he knew that wouldn't be enough.

"Jack! It's good to see you." Diane Piletti greeted him at the door like a long-lost friend. "How's everything at the store? Hope you're as busy as we are."

Taken aback by her enthusiasm, Jack mumbled a few niceties. Then he glanced around the floor. "Is Mary around?"

Diane's face brightened even more. "Of course she is. I'll tell her you're here. Better yet, why don't you go ahead into the office," she said, taking him by the arm. "She's paying bills right now, so I'm sure she won't mind a break. She'll be glad to see you."

He doubted that highly.

The grinning Diane abandoned him at the closed office door, leaving him to announce his own presence. He took a deep breath, knocked once on the door and then let himself in.

"Hi, Mary."

Her entire body stiffened at the sound of his voice. Slowly she lifted her gaze from the checkbook spread out on her desk. She looked so damn good—too damn good. With her dark hair combed back with sleek gold combs, her eyes seemed even softer and her face fresh and alive. He couldn't help remembering how warm and lovely she was, asleep in his bed this morning. She had looked so peaceful, he couldn't bear to disturb her with the painful realization that had kept him awake half the night. Not then, anyway.

"What do you want?"

Clearly she was angry and, as far as he was concerned, she had every right to be. "We need to talk about us."

"I don't need to."

"I do."

"Then by all means," she said with an exaggerated sweep of her arm toward the empty chair. "Let's not keep you from what you need."

Her sarcasm scraped his heart; it wasn't like her. But it was his fault, and he planned to put a stop to it right now. Closing the door behind him, he ignored the proffered seat. Instead he stood before her, prepared to begin the hardest thing he'd ever had to do: let her go.

"This business with my family has been rough these last few days. Really rough," he began, trying to capture her gaze. But she deliberately looked past him. "Still, when I decided to come back to Springfield, I made a promise to myself to see it through no matter what kind of flack I might get. This trouble with Peter is pretty bad, but I'm committed to working it out. As I see it, I have no choice."

"Aren't you the one who said we do our own choosing?"

"I've said a lot of dumb things lately, including the statement that you'd be better off staying here."

Mary's gold green eyes flashed to attention, focusing on him at last.

"You see, I'd forgotten what it feels like to want to break out of the familiar, to face new challenges and prove myself. But that's why I left twenty years ago, isn't it?"

Her expression softened a bit. "So you've told me."

"Considering that and what happened with my brother, I'd be a fool to keep discounting why you want to pursue your opportunity in Boston," he admitted, hoping she realized how much he meant it. "And I have to stop blinding myself to your restlessness with Springfield, or you'll end up hating me, too. I couldn't take that, Mary."

"I do get angry with you, Jack. Somehow it never lasts long," she added with gentle exasperation. "And I could never hate you."

"Give resentment enough time and anything can happen."

"Jack—"

"Let me go on, please." He pressed his palms flat on her desk and leaned closer. "Look, last night—for a while—I thought for sure we'd come together for keeps this time. Somehow we were going to be fine."

Mary winced. "So did I."

"Yeah? And how did you think our, ah, problem was going to be resolved?"

"We'd compromise. Figure a way to split our time between here and there."

"And until I came to my senses, I was so sure you'd finally realized you belonged in Springfield, with me." He pushed away from the desk and her disappointed eyes. "Don't you see, Mary? We're running around in circles, but we're not even on the same track."

She came to his side. "What would be so terrible about working something out? Just tell me. People manage long-distance relationships all the time. And you yourself said Boston isn't that far away."

"It's not a proper way to build a life together. I don't care how many people do it. This kiss-me-goodbye-on-Monday-I'll-see-you-on-Friday stuff is not for me. I moved back to get a whole life, to have a real family." He turned to her, gripping her shoulders with his hands, wishing he could make her see. "Look, Sandra and I lived in the same house, and our marriage still fell apart because we had no time for each other."

"I am not Sandra!" She swung away, crossing her arms across her chest.

"No, you're Mary Piletti, the best person I know, and you have every right to get what you want. And it's time we both got on with our new lives."

"Just like that?" Mary's gaze flickered with uncertainty, as if his adamance had caught her off guard. Then he realized she, too, was having a tough time letting go.

He swallowed hard and delivered a verbal shove. "Do you want to give up your partnership?"

She stared at him with wide, moist eyes, and it took all his strength to keep from folding her in his arms. In the end, however, she shook her head no. Although it was the answer he'd expected, it still cut through him like a cold steel blade. He turned to leave.

"Now I feel selfish," she said, her voice shaky.

Opening the office door, he paused to reassure her one last time. "Believe me, Mary, after all these years, you deserve to be a little selfish."

Chapter Twelve

The first day of October was unseasonably chilly, bordering on cold. As soon as she arrived at Twice as Nice, Mary switched on the thermostat, then shivered as she started a pot of coffee brewing. It was eight o'clock in the morning. The shop didn't open until ten, but here she was because she hadn't slept well—again.

Since she'd returned from Boston two weeks earlier, her days had been hectic, her nights restless. She kept busy during the day with the store and preparations for the move. She spent the evenings trying not to think about Jack and what might have been, which rarely led to a peaceful night's sleep. But that would cease being a problem once she was out of Springfield for good. She was sure of it.

Coffee mug in hand, Mary went out onto the floor to sift through the racks for the green-tagged garments slated for the markdown corner. She nearly jumped out of her skin with fright when she spotted the black-clothed, hulking figure pressed against the front glass door, knocking. After a nervous second look, Mary recognized Angie Candelaria.

"What on earth," she muttered, hurrying to unlock the door for Jack's aunt.

"Mary, I'm barging in, I know," Angie declared in her deep-voiced bellow. "But it couldn't be helped."

"It's so early." She helped Angie take off her heavy black wool coat. "How did you know I'd be here?"

"I was out walking Pepino and I saw you drive by. I figured you were on the way here. I tossed Pepi back into the house and came in my car."

This had to be serious—everyone knew Angie only drove between the hours of ten and three. Mary sat the old woman in the cushioned chair next to the checkout counter and fetched her a cup of coffee. Angie accepted it gratefully, patting her hand. "You're a good girl, Mary. Have I apologized for the way I spoke to you at Rose's that night?"

"Well . . . no." Mary hadn't seen her since that tumultuous family dinner at the Candelarias'.

"I didn't know how to take such straight talk from a young woman like you. But never mind that." Angie patted her hand again. "It proves you're strong, and that's why I came. I need your help."

"What on earth for?" This surprise request for help overshadowed the realization that Angie still hadn't apologized to her.

Fat tears welled up in Angie's severe black eyes. "For my family—for Rose and the boys. My poor Vito's family is in ruins. There may even be a—a—divorce."

Angie began crying in earnest, and Mary was astounded. This was the last thing she was expecting—though the unexpected was becoming routine fare for the Candelarias. She fumbled beneath the counter for some tissues and gently offered them to the distraught woman.

"They're all I have in this world. I have no husband, no children," Angie continued between sobs. "Rose is so cold to me—not that I blame her. I've caused trouble, I know." She dabbed her wet face with a tissue. "Gina and the babies are gone. Peter is in misery. And Jack...well, you know Jack and I don't speak. This is my fault, too."

Mary wondered how this amazing change of heart came about. Had the possible self-destruction of Angie's family really made her see the error of her ways? Stranger things had happened.

"Have you tried talking to Jack at all?" she asked. "You might be surprised."

Angie turned pale. "No, I couldn't. I'm too embarrassed to ask for his forgiveness. You've heard the things I said about him. Besides, I thought maybe you could talk to him for me. Ask him to go bring Gina back for his brother, or at least fix it so she'll come home."

"Me? I'm the last person Jack wants to hear from."

"You are? But I thought..."

She knew what Angie thought. In fact, Angie had been convinced she and Jack were a couple way before it had seemed even remotely possible to them.

"In any case, Angie, Jack can't bring Gina back. That's up to Peter."

"I suppose you're right. Maybe you could talk to Peter? I've tried, but he's beside himself. He's so angry. And I think he's scared to death he'll never see his beautiful babies again. Please, Mary, I don't know who else to turn to for help." Angie's tears flowed once more. "You know, every day after Mass, I say the rosary for all of them—Rose . . . Gina . . . Peter . . . even Jack."

The rosary business did Mary in. The fact that the indomitable Angie Candelaria was sobbing right in front of her didn't help, either. How could she turn the woman away?

"Angie, I'll make a deal with you. If you promise to go see Jack, today, and try to make up with him, then I'll see what I can do about Peter. Maybe my father can reason with him."

Angie seemed uncertain at first. "You think Jack will even see me?"

"I know he will." Mary bit back a smile. She'd give anything to see the look on Jack's face when Angie showed up to reconcile.

"I'll go to his bicycle store at lunchtime. I'll bring him a sandwich—and some of my apple cake. He loved it when he was a little boy."

Buoyed by her new mission, Angie maneuvered her bulky body up from the chair. She thanked Mary repeatedly as she buttoned her coat and wrapped a dark scarf around her head. "It's too bad you and Jack didn't get together," Angie added, blunt as ever. "He could use a good, strong-minded girl like you to keep him in line."

From noontime on, Mary found it impossible to keep her thoughts from wandering across town to the bicycle shop and the reunion scenario she hoped was being played out there. Even a call from a Boston property management company, about an upcoming vacancy in the apartment building she had liked, offered little distraction. Although she was happy to make arrangements to view the efficiency apartment over the weekend, her attention quickly returned to how things might've fared between Angie and Jack.

She decided to stop by her parents' house after work, just in case any news had come down via the Peek Street grapevine. This time, curiosity overrode her usual scorn for that particular pipeline.

Pulling up to the house, she noticed Peter Candelaria's car was still parked in the office driveway. Since it was almost six-thirty, Mary knew Charlie had gone home, meaning Peter was probably alone. She thought about her promise to Angie. Because Peter seemed to view her as something akin to a pesky little sister, she had intended to ask her father to talk to him. Yet opportunity was presenting itself here and now.

Why not try? After all, Angie Candelaria didn't come begging for help every day.

In the office Peter stood hunched over the copy machine, its rumbling hum obliterating the sound of her arrival. Mary watched him feed documents into the copier, unaware of her presence. He was shorter than Jack, slighter, too, though he possessed the same warm Candelaria coloring. Only on him it wasn't as vivid. The same could be said of Peter's personality, too, and perhaps, that contributed to his antipathy for Jack. As far as she could tell, Peter had always been overshadowed by his older brother—even during the many years Jack hadn't been around. The opinions may have been negative, but it was always "Jack this" and "Jack that."

"Hi, Peter."

He glanced up from the machine. "Charlie's already gone home."

"Yeah, I know." She strolled over to the copy machine. "You planning on working late?"

"Beats going home to an empty house."

She placed a sympathetic hand on his arm. "Is there something I can do to help? Do you need someone to talk to?"

"The last person I need to talk to is my brother's new best friend." Jerking his arm away, Peter turned off the copier and gathered the stack of documents. "Oh, but I forgot," he added, plopping the papers on his desk. "You two are on the outs, aren't you? Maybe we do have something to commiserate about, after all."

"In an odd sort of way, I guess." Had she made a mistake in coming here? She'd forgotten just how belligerent Peter could be.

"I'll tell you what's odd—that you and Jack had a fling in the first place. I never would've figured him to be your type. Then again, slick charm and lots of money can mask a multitude of sins—up to a point." Sitting at the desk, Peter propped his hand under his chin. "Glad to see you've finally come to your senses."

Mary stared at him in disbelief. "You just refuse to cut Jack a break. You're never going to give him a chance, are you?"

"Why should I?"

"Haven't you ever heard of forgive and forget?"

"Jack was trouble twenty years ago, and he's trouble now," asserted Peter. "Who the hell does he think he is to come waltzing back into town, stirring everybody up, and telling me what to do?"

"He's a man who wants his family back."

"Oh, that's a load of bull." Peter tugged off his necktie and threw it on the desk. "He's the reason I'm sitting here in this lousy office at seven o'clock at night with no one to go home to. Because of him I lost my family. It's because of him I got stuck here in the first place."

"Are you ever going to take responsibility for your own life?" Shaking her head, Mary stepped up to his desk and tossed her purse down. "From what I see, the only person keeping you stuck here is you, and the only thing holding you back is your own self-doubt. You're afraid you can't make it on your own. Except it's so much easier to blame Jack, isn't it?"

"Nice speech, Mary. Sounds like Jack taught you well."

"Oh, Peter," she said, groaning, "grow up."

He leaned back in his swivel chair, looking the picture of calm—save for the storm brewing in his brown eyes. "You know, I always thought we had a lot in common. We both have had our share of family responsibilities—heavy ones that tied us down to Peek

Street, kept us trapped. But you'll be leaving us soon, won't you?"

"So?"

"So preaching seems to come easy to you, now that your situation is changing. Nothing's gonna stop you now, right Mary? Family can't hold you back anymore. Why, even the fact that my brother would marry you in a minute can't make you stay in Springfield."

She felt as if she'd been punched. "You—you don't know what you're talking about."

"The whole street knows about you and Jack."

"Well, I don't care, and neither should you," she snapped. "But before I leave, maybe I should give you something more important to think about than my relationship with Jack."

"More preaching?"

"Just chew on this, my friend—sometimes traps are of our own making and exist only in our minds." She picked up her purse from the desk, hiking the strap onto her shoulder. "You'd be a fool not to take Jack up on his offer, no matter what the risk. And even if you should happen to fail, you won't have to muddle through alone. Your family will be there for you—including your wife and brother."

"Sure you won't change your mind, Leo?" Jack asked, strapping a bike into place on his car roof rack.

"Nah. I've got to get the workroom cleaned up." Leo gestured back at the shop. "Then I'm going to hit that fiddle festival up in Northampton. You're welcome to come along."

"Thanks, but I'm in the mood to ride today." And in the mood for some companionship. But Leo had been his last hope, so now he seemed fated to go it alone. Pulling out of the parking lot, Jack headed west with no particular destination in mind. All he wanted was a long stretch of road on which to breeze along, riding the nagging restlessness out of his system.

The highway into the Berkshires was buzzing with traffic, and Jack remembered this was the weekend that the area's fall foliage was to reach peak color. The roads would be jammed. He pulled off at the nearest exit, only to realize it was close to the route he had ridden with Mary weeks ago. It wasn't exactly the ride he had in mind when he'd started out, but now he figured why the hell not? Mary was at the root of his restlessness, and she was just about always on his mind, anyway—especially after Aunt Angie's surprise visit.

Maybe one good wallow would do the trick to help cleanse Miss Mary from his soul.

The air was brisk and the autumn sun felt good on his back as he rode the familiar route. The car traffic on these winding back roads was mercifully light, although he was pleased to encounter quite a few fellow cyclists along the way. He pedaled on, now and then flashing back to that wonderful ride with Mary. When he reached the base of the steep hill leading to Splendor Bluff, he couldn't help chuckling at the memory of Mary attacking that hill with jokes and determination.

Had that been when he'd realized he was crazy about her? And that every other woman on this planet would pale in comparison?

The view from atop the bluff was even more dazzling, now that the blanket of green had turned into a blazing quilt of orange and gold patchwork. But the view brought Jack no pleasure. His only thought was how he wanted to bring Mary back to share this. He had promised himself he would.

He felt hollow inside, and it was clear he'd been a fool to stop at Splendor Bluff today. Being here alone only pressed home the question that'd been haunting him for weeks: what kind of life could he have in Springfield without her?

He could kick himself for thinking like that. What was wrong with him? He was home, finally home after years of what amounted to exile—self-imposed or otherwise. Gradually he was starting to reconnect with the community. The situation with Peter was still dicey, but, wonder of wonders, Aunt Angie had begun to come around. When she had marched into his shop, sputtering apologies and giving him food, words couldn't describe his elation. Angie's visit reinforced his hope that someday soon he would attain a normal family relationship.

Yet, as he stood at this breathtaking spot, that elation, that hope, that feeling of home had all but evaporated. Somehow, it all took a back seat to Mary. Jack shook his head at the irony. Because of her, his faith in himself and in happiness had been renewed. Only now he felt adrift, and he certainly wasn't happy.

Fate was playing one hell of a joke on him.

The sound of laughter echoed behind him, and Jack turned to see a man and a woman walking with their bicycles toward the bluff. Nodding to him as they passed by, the twenty-something couple leaned the bikes against the gray boulder before strolling off, arm in arm, to admire the view.

"They call this spot Splendor Bluff," said the young man, drawing the blonde closer to his side.

She put her head on his shoulder. "I can see why."

Feeling out of place, and maybe a bit old, Jack pedaled away. So much for Splendor Bluff. Spurned lovers, like himself, did not belong there. And one good "wallow" wasn't going to cure him of Mary Piletti. Only time could do that.

Deciding to call it quits for the day, he rode back to the car and then drove home. When he pulled up to the apartment building, he wondered—as he always did—if he'd bump into Mary. Not that that had happened in the last two weeks, which was something to marvel at considering they lived in the same building. Or maybe not. He imagined Mary would be damn good at deliberately avoiding him—if she'd set her mind to it. Inside, as he'd suspected, the main floor corridor was quiet and empty. Mary's door was closed tight. Once again he told himself not to take it as a personal affront, no matter how shut out it made him feel.

Upon reaching the third floor, he noticed someone sitting on the carpet outside his apartment door. He squinted against the dim, yellowish cast of the hall ceiling lamp, and realized it was Peter. After his initial surprise, Jack wasn't sure how he felt. His brother had actually come to him, a notable first. Yet, he was in no mood for yet another run-in with Peter. Not today.

Peter got to his feet. "Hi. Hope you don't mind me waiting here for you."

"No, but Mary probably would've let you in. She has a master key."

"I tried. She's not home."

Jack unlocked the door. "Come on in, then."

Peter followed him inside, silent and appearing ill at ease. Jack didn't know what to make of it. What had compelled his brother to sit and wait for him like that? Why was he here at all? He supposed he just should be grateful Peter hadn't immediately started chewing him out.

"Can I get you something? Soda? Beer?"

"Nothing, thanks."

Then Peter just stood there, as if he was waiting for Jack to make the first move. Figuring it probably took up all of his kid brother's initiative to come here, Jack sensed he needed to nudge things along.

"Why don't we sit down?" He pointed to the sofa. "And then you can tell me what's up."

Without so much as a word, Peter moved to the couch. He seemed so awkward and stiff, Jack felt sorry for him.

"Okay, Pete, I give up. Why are you here?"

Peter stared down at his hands, his nervous fingers moving nonstop. "To talk about your business offer. Are you still interested in that?"

"I am if you are."

"Seems to be the only way I'm gonna get my wife and kids back," he said with a shrug.

It wasn't the most enthusiastic of acceptances, but Jack was willing to take it. "It's a start, brother, it's a start."

"Were you serious about being a hands-off, silent partner?"

"Absolutely. I've got my own business to run. Not that I'm giving out blank checks, mind you. But I trust you to keep things in line."

"Even after everything that's gone down between us?"

"That's personal. This is business. Mario speaks highly of your abilities. He thinks you're more than capable of building up your own company."

Finally Peter relaxed a bit. He leaned back into the sofa cushions. "It wasn't easy coming over here today."

"I noticed."

"Made me realize how really hard coming back to Springfield must've been."

"Not exactly a day at the beach," Jack said, forcing himself to sound casual, although he was taken aback by Peter's remark. It was the last thing he'd expected to hear.

"While I was waiting outside for you, I got to thinking about how alone I've felt these last few weeks—what with everyone treating me like the world's biggest jerk. Gina left me, Mom's upset, the looks I get on the street, and the gossip!" Peter added with disbelief. "It hit me that it's the same kind of treatment you've been getting for years. I don't know how you stood it."

Trying to keep himself out of shock, Jack shrugged and muttered, "Got used to it."

"No one gets used to that, not even you." Peter shook his head. "You took it because you wanted your family back—just like Mary said."

"Mary said what?"

"Plenty, believe me. She came into my office the other night and got on my case big-time about you."

"Mary gave you a hard time about me?" First she got Angie over to his store, and now Peter...what was it with her?

"Ah, she really let me have it. But you know Mary, she doesn't mess around."

"Yeah, best to mind your p's and q's with Miss Mary." Recalling the time she scolded the two of them for fighting in her apartment building, he couldn't help smiling. "The schoolteacher in her never died, you know."

Peter gave him a questioning look. "You've got it bad, don't you?"

"I'll get over it." He had to.

"She's really going to leave?"

"Looks that way."

"Women. They can really do us guys in."

"But your woman's coming back to you, Pete, I'm sure of it."

Grateful to be sharing something other than animosity with him, Jack gazed at his kid brother. Brotherly affection—long missed, never forgotten—sprouted in him anew. He hoped Peter felt the same way.

"How about something to eat before we sit down and talk business? Aunt Angie brought me an apple cake, and I can put on a pot of coffee."

"Aunt Angie's apple cake? Sounds good." Peter's lips twitched into a sly smile. "She's come around, eh?"

"What can I say? I'm on a roll."

* * *

Jack knew he was taking a chance.

His welcome might be less than cordial, the conversation strained, but he had to go through with it. Whatever her reasons, whatever her methods, Mary had managed to push Peter and Aunt Angie back into his camp, and he owed her a great deal of thanks. That's why he'd come—to give her a proper thank-you, face-to-face, from the heart. No strings, certainly no expectations. Clutching the bouquet of fall flowers he'd picked out at the florist's, he took a deep breath and marched through the doors of Twice as Nice.

It appeared to be a slow morning as there wasn't a customer in sight. But Monday mornings were usually slow at his place, too. He scanned the store for Mary, but only spotted her sister-in-law, Diane, hanging up baby clothes at the other end of the shop. When Josephine Piletti emerged from the office, however, second thoughts about coming boomeranged through his mind.

"Jackie! What a nice surprise." She zeroed in on the bouquet. "And what do we have here?"

He peered down at the short, plump woman who was gazing up at him with what seemed like stars in her eyes, and felt trapped. "I—ah—I brought these..."

"For Mary?"

"Well, yes."

Josephine called over her shoulder to her daughter-in-law. "Diane, come see the beautiful flowers Jack brought Mary."

The younger woman bustled to the front of the store. "Oh, my, how lovely."

"Aren't they gorgeous?" Josephine said, nodding her head with approval. "Mary's going to love them, isn't she, Diane?"

"Of course she will."

"She'll be thrilled," Josephine added, "just thrilled."

Jack turned to Diane. "Mary isn't here?"

"Why, no." She seemed startled. "Didn't Joseph—"

"I haven't had a chance, yet." Josephine shot Diane a scolding look. "Mary's not here at the moment, Jack. But when she sees these, I know she's gonna want to thank you right away."

"That's not necessary."

"Oh, but she'll want to, I know. Mary adores flowers. But you probably already know that, don't you?" Josephine reached for the bouquet in his hands. "Let me go put these in water so they'll be fresh as new when Mary gets back. Which should be any time now," she added hastily.

After giving Diane another meaningful look, Josephine took the bouquet back into the office.

"So where is Mary really, Diane? In spite of what Josephine says, I get the impression she's not just running an errand down the street."

Diane shrugged and stared down at her hands.

"She's in Boston, right?"

With a sigh she glanced back at the office door. "I'm going to get spanked for this, but I guess you have a right to know."

He knew it. "She's in Boston."

"Just for the weekend. We really do expect her back this afternoon," Diane explained. "She went to look at an apartment. She liked it well enough, so she stayed until this morning to sign a lease.''

An apartment...a lease...not unexpected news by any means. So why was it hitting him like a ton of bricks? Damn! He'd only come to deliver flowers. Yet, as he left Mary's store, he knew he had another round of heavy soul-searching to do.

Chapter Thirteen

Mary's parents were waiting for her to help set up for their annual neighborhood Columbus Day party, and she was running late. Yet, on her way out the door, the flowers on the coffee table caught her eye. She stopped and sighed. The week-old arrangement had wilted and dried, and it was beyond time to throw it out. Dead flowers, dead relationship. So why did tossing them make her feel sad?

She shook her head, remembering how her heart had leapt with hope when she'd returned from Boston to find the flowers on her desk. Had Jack reconsidered? Was he willing to work things out after all? But his message on the florist's card had simply thanked her for helping with Peter and Angie. It was a thoughtful gesture on Jack's part, and she truly was glad she had helped the Candelarias reconcile. Trouble was, she'd wanted Jack's flowers to mean something different.

But they hadn't. The card may have said thank you, yet the message felt coldly the same: be with him on his terms or forget it.

Damn him! And damn these flowers. She should've gotten rid of them that first day. She never should've brought them home. Still, they'd been too beautiful to throw away... and they were from Jack. She took the vase into the kitchen. Dropping the withered bouquet into the wastebasket helped her feel better. But not much.

She wished her feelings weren't in such a jumble. Anger. Sadness. Love. Hate. It was enough to make her scream. God, she was glad she'd rented the apartment in Boston. The sooner she moved out of Springfield the better. And it wouldn't be long now. Her lawyer and the Michaels' lawyer had worked out the final terms, and contracts were being drafted. If all went well, the contracts would arrive for her to sign by the end of the week.

When she got to her parents' house, Charlie and his gang were already there helping. This was the family's fifteenth Columbus Day party, and everyone had their jobs down pat. By the time two o'clock and the first guests rolled in, the backyard was gaily decorated with green, white and orange streamers and Italian flags. Folding tables were laden with pasta, pastries and punch. It was a warm, sunny mid-October Sunday; a last gasp of Indian summer that heightened Mary's sense of closure. A part of her life was coming to an end, and soon she'd be nothing more than a visitor to these scenes of family, community and tradition.

At three, Rose and Angie Candelaria arrived. Rose handed Mary a large platter of cannelloni as Josephine greeted both women with hugs and kisses.

"Where's Peter?" Josephine asked.

"He went to New Hampshire to see Gina and the kids," Rose said. "Jack dropped us off."

"Dropped you off? For goodness' sake, isn't he coming?"

Suddenly it got very quiet, and Mary felt everyone's eyes on her.

Josephine called to Charlie. "See if you can catch Jack. Get him to come back."

Charlie glanced at Mary, shrugged and then hurried off around the house. He shouted out Jack's name, and within seconds she heard a car door slam. Jack was coming.

She got busy straightening one of the dessert tables—the one farthest away from where Jack would be entering the backyard. Yet when he walked in with Charlie, her gaze was drawn to him like a magnet. Wearing a dark green pullover sweater and tan slacks, he was a sight for sore eyes. Her heart felt like it was doing acrobatics inside her chest, while every nerve in her body tensed. Still, seeing him again made her feel lonely.

But, for her own good, she had to stay away from him.

Her mother, Rose and Angie were on him like flies, chatting and laughing, getting him a beer, bringing him food. Not once did he look around for her. Grabbing a half-empty punch bowl, she stalked off into the haven of her mother's kitchen. As she poured more ginger ale and juice into the crystal bowl, her father came in holding an unopened bottle of red wine.

"Dickie Ladero just brought this back from Sicily. I thought we'd drink it now," Mario said as he shuffled through the counter drawers. "Where'd your mother hide my corkscrew?"

"It's right there on the kitchen table, Dad."

He reached for the corkscrew and then plunked the bottle down on the counter, next to where she was working. "How come you're hiding in the kitchen?"

"I'm not hiding. I'm making more punch."

"Oh? Sorry." Squinting hard, he twisted and yanked at the cork until it popped from the bottle. He studied the cork for a moment and then looked over at her. "Jack's here you know."

"I know."

"Aren't you going to come out and say hello? I'm sure he's wondering where you are."

Mary stiffened. "I will—after I finish up here."

"Want me to send him in?"

"No, I don't." She pointed at the window over the sink. "He's having a great time talking to Danny Tucci and Angie. Let him be."

Although he seemed reluctant, her father agreed and went back outside with Dickie Ladero's wine.

When she finished replenishing the punch, even more people had arrived at the party, making it easier for her to get lost in the crowd. She knew she should at least say hello to Jack, and she would—later. For the moment, however, she was happily dragged into a conversation about children's clothes by several of

Diane's friends. When that broke up, she poured herself a glass of wine and headed for the front yard. As she'd hoped, no one was about.

Finally allowing herself to relax, she sank into one of the white lawn chairs, sipped Dickie Ladero's wine and basked in the warmth of the autumn sun on her skin. She needed this moment of peace and quiet.

"Hi."

With her heart in her throat, she looked up. "Hi, Jack."

"I don't like to intrude on your privacy," he said without a trace of his usual warmth, "but my mother insists I apologize to you for being rude."

"Rude how?"

"For not speaking to you. Of course, she doesn't realize you've been avoiding me all afternoon."

"Sorry, but I've been too busy helping with the party to avoid anybody—including you." She thought she sounded convincing. "Besides, why would I avoid you when I've been wanting to thank you for the lovely flowers?"

"Oh? Well, there's no need to thank me for a thank-you gift." Then his tone softened. "It was a heartfelt thank-you, by the way."

She looked away. "So, Peter's come around?"

"Starting to, anyway. We've talked once, and we plan to again when he gets back from seeing Gina. Nothing's settled, though."

"At least you're talking."

"Because of you. Whatever you said to him seemed to have an amazing effect. And Angie, too. You could've knocked me over with a feather when she waltzed into the shop."

"Angie was ready. All she needed was a little push."

"Well, I appreciate it, and I'm glad you got the flowers."

She nodded and smiled, not really knowing how else to respond. It was awful. Their conversation was so stiff, she felt uncomfortable. And she never would've believed talking to Jack could be this difficult.

"I hear you've rented a place in Boston," Jack said, breaking the awkward silence.

"How did you know?"

"Diane told me—when I delivered the flowers," he explained. "That was awfully quick, wasn't it?"

She stiffened, feeling defensive. "It was in a building I liked, and the apartment itself was great. I didn't want to risk losing it."

"I see. Now you're—"

"Jack! There you are." Charlie called, bounding into the front yard, wedging himself between Mary and Jack. "An old friend of yours is here and she's dying to see you—Debbie Waslewski—from high school."

Jack looked mystified. "Debbie Waslewski?"

"Debbie Panetta before she got married. Remember? You took her to the senior prom," Charlie added, nudging Jack toward the backyard. "I promised her I'd find you right away. She's waiting by the soda cooler."

"Mary and I are talking right now."

Charlie waved this off. "You don't mind, do you, Mare?"

Not trusting herself to sound convincing this time, she simply shook her head no.

He stared at her for a moment, his gaze cool. "Fine. I guess I'll see you both around."

Mary watched him disappear behind the house, then she rose from the lawn chair to confront her brother. "Debbie Waslewski? Why did you sic her on Jack?" The woman had just divorced her second husband and was definitely on the prowl for number three.

Startled by her vehemence, Charlie hunched his shoulders in self-defense. "Because they dated in high school, and she's anxious to see him again."

"I just bet she is."

He shot her a puzzled look. "Hey, I really did this to help you out. I saw Jack follow you here—in fact everybody saw Jack follow you here. Since you two split up, I figured you didn't want him hassling you. Was I wrong?"

"No, I guess not." She sighed and sank back into the chair. "What did you mean by 'everybody saw'?"

"Mom and Dad, mostly. And Rose and Angie."

"Great, just great." She drank the last of her wine.

"Look at it this way—now they'll all be buzzing about Jack and Debbie."

This didn't sit well with her, although heaven knew why. "At least that foolishness about me and Jack being engaged didn't get out. Why you and Diane got that notion I'll never—" The sheepish expression on her brother's face stopped her cold. "Charlie—did you tell someone?"

He took a deep breath. "Dad."

"Dad?" Disbelieving, she rubbed her forehead with her hand. "Why did you do a thing like that?"

"Because I thought it was true, and it was before Diane called to tell me it wasn't," he explained, sit-

ting down on the ground beside her chair. "But you
don't have to worry. As soon as I heard from Diane, I
told Dad I was wrong, that I'd jumped to the wrong
conclu—"

"You didn't tell him Jack and I—ah—you know."

"Spent the night together? Come on, Mare—give
me credit for some discretion."

"Sorry."

"You don't have to worry about this. I convinced
him it was all a mistake and that it'd be very embarrassing to you and Jack if anything was said."

"And he bought that?"

"Absolutely. Has he said anything to you?"

"No, he hasn't." Except for trying to push her out
of the kitchen to talk to Jack earlier this afternoon...which he probably would've done anyway. In
fact, she hadn't given his prompting a second thought.

"I even convinced him not to say anything to Mom
about it," Charlie added. "You know this kind of
thing would make her crazy."

"Please, don't remind me." She shook her head,
feeling as if she'd escaped untold hassles by the skin of
her teeth.

"Of course it doesn't mean they've given up on you
and Jack. There was a definite reason Mom sent me
chasing after Jack earlier."

"That was obvious."

Charlie looked up at her, his expression thoughtful. "I haven't given up hope, either, you know. Jack's
turned out to be a swell guy."

"Jack is a swell guy. But . . ." Thinking of the cool
distance she'd just felt between them, Mary swal-

lowed hard to keep her voice from cracking. "But he's not the guy for me."

Returning from the Pilettis, Jack parked in front of his building and sat in the car, staring at the front door. He'd reached the point where he hated coming here. It wasn't home anymore, it was a reminder of Mary, a reminder of loss. Walking past Mary's closed door felt like a stab in the chest, a sharp and lingering pain that was impossible to ease.

Why couldn't he find a house to buy, so he could get the hell out of here? Anything should do, the way he was feeling these days. Only he couldn't bring himself to commit to just any house. Nothing suited him. Every property paled in comparison to the Feeney house—as much as he hated to admit it. He didn't need or want that white elephant, and Sally Feeney had taken it off the market, anyway. Yet he couldn't get it off his mind. In a way, it was just another reminder of Mary.

Damn! Jack slammed his palms against the steering wheel. He wished Mario had never shown him that house. And he wished Mary had left Springfield three months sooner—before they ever had a chance to become involved. Then there wouldn't have been this pain...

He dragged himself out of the car. Maybe he should've had that drink Debbie Waslewski offered when he'd dropped her off after the party. They had a lot of years to catch up on, and despite the years, Debbie had kept her good looks—still blond, curvy and eager to please. And a tad desperate, he thought sadly. Trouble was, he was feeling desperate himself.

Why inflict that on her? Nothing good could come of it.

She wasn't Mary.

He puttered aimlessly around his apartment, picking up scattered glasses and dishes, poking in the refrigerator for sandwich makings. He gave a start when the ringing telephone shattered the lonely quiet, and he was surprised that it was Peter calling.

"I just got back from New Hampshire, but Ma's not here," Peter said. "She with you?"

"She stayed on at the Pilettis' party. Mario's taking her home," he explained. "So, how'd things go with Gina?"

"Good. Really good. We talked a lot, and I think she's ready to come back. Maybe in a week or two."

"Great, Pete. You don't know how glad I am to hear that."

"You don't know how glad I am to say it. It's been tough," he said. "Look, I'm feeling kind of restless right now. Would you—ah—be interested in meeting me for a beer?"

"Now? Ah, I don't know. I'm pretty tired." Jack could scarcely believe what he was saying. A few weeks ago, he would've jumped at the chance to have a beer with his brother—especially since Peter was doing the inviting. Not that he wasn't pleased now. It just didn't feel as compelling. Nothing did. "Sorry, Pete. But it's been a long afternoon."

"You went to the Pilettis' party, too?"

"You've got it."

"Things weren't so good with Mary?"

Reminded of Mary's coolness, Jack took a deep breath. "She barely gave me the time of day."

"Must've been rough."

"It's over, man—I knew that." And pushed for it, too. They each had to get on with their lives. That was what he'd wanted, wasn't it? And Mary certainly hadn't wasted any time in finding an apartment in Boston. "It's for the best," he told Peter.

Maybe it was in the long run, but for now, it was just plain awful.

"Sorry about that, Jack. Is there anything I can do?"

"Yeah, there is. Meet me for that beer, after all," Jack said, realizing being alone was the last thing he needed. At least now he had his brother to fall back on. "I'll see you at Tony's in ten minutes."

After work on Saturday, Mary drove to her parents' house to pick up her partnership contracts, which had just been delivered by an overnight express service. She'd asked that the contracts be sent to her folks' place because someone would be there to receive them. She didn't want to chance missing a delivery to the shop or her apartment. Now that the contracts had arrived safely, all she had to do was review them, sign them and send them back to Boston on Monday morning.

"Hmm. Smells good," she said when she walked into the kitchen. She gave her mother a peck on the cheek. "What's for supper?"

"Pot roast and vegetables." Josephine gave the contents of the heavy iron pot on the stove a good stir. "Want to stay?"

"Love to." Even though she'd be back tomorrow afternoon for Sunday dinner, Mary figured she'd get as much of her mother's great cooking while she could. It was one thing—among many—she'd miss when she moved to Boston.

"Your father went down the street to visit Dickie Ladero. We'll eat when he gets back."

"Fine. Ah, where are the contracts?"

"On Dad's desk out in the office." Josephine frowned, shaking her head. "He was not happy to get that package. That's why I sent him down to Dickie's, to get his mind off it."

"That bad, huh?"

"He was tempted to throw them out. But I said, 'Mario, she's a grown woman. She's going to do what she's going to do.' It's just that he hates to see you go."

"I know he does. And I feel sad about it in a way, too. But I wouldn't be doing this if I didn't think it was for the best."

"I guess you're right." With a sigh, her mother began tearing lettuce leaves into a large wooden salad bowl. "Go ahead and look at your papers. I'll call you when it's time to eat."

Mary gave her mother an affectionate pat on the back before heading into the real estate office. Now that her days in Springfield were dwindling, every conversation was laced with emotions poignant, ambiguous and sentimental. Each "so long" and "see you later" might be the last for a long while. True, she wasn't moving to Alaska, and she'd visit home often. But after living in this one town her entire life, it wouldn't be the same. Nothing would be the same.

She didn't even know if she'd see Jack again before she moved. Their encounter at the Columbus Day party would be a disappointing way to end what was—

for her, at least—a significant relationship. One moment she longed to say a proper goodbye to him, to mend the hard feelings, to part as friends. The next moment she realized how impossible that would be. Coward that she was, she didn't dare seek him out. The feelings between them were dangerous—still hot to the touch. The resentments were too strong.

Finding the express service package on her father's desk, she sat down and began to read the contract. Although these papers were integral to her future, Mary was finding it difficult to give them the detailed reading they deserved. Too many distractions for her to concentrate...her parents...her new apartment...her favorite customers at the store...the new store...and Jack, above all.

The door leading to the house creaked behind her, and she turned to find her father standing on the threshold.

"Hi, Dad. Supper ready?"

He shook his head. "I need to talk to you, Mary."

"Sure." Resigned to the inevitability of this talk, Mary pulled up a chair for her father.

"Your mother thinks we should keep our noses out of this, and she is probably right," he said gruffly. "And I wouldn't say anything at all if the circumstances were different, but honey, you shouldn't go away now."

"What do you mean if circumstances were different?"

But he continued as if he hadn't heard her. "You don't realize how precious time is. It can pass so quickly. The years are gone before you know it."

"Dad, what are you talking about?"

"Jack."

"Jack?"

"And you."

"Oh, Dad." She sank deeper into her chair.

"Something has to be said. We have all been tip-toeing around you two, waiting for one of you to come to your senses. I had hopes . . . then that came." He waved a hand at the contract on his desk with disgust.

"*That* is very important to me."

"More important than a husband, children, a home?"

"Aren't you jumping the gun a little? Jack isn't about to—"

"I know all about Jack." Mario got to his feet and began pacing in front of her. "But he has proven his worth these last few months. He has grown up to be the kind of man I want for my daughter. Besides, when he came back, you didn't believe the rumors and the gossip about him. You saw through all that."

"Look, just because I saw he wasn't the dishonor-able scoundrel the neighborhood had vilified all these years, doesn't mean we're destined to be together."

"Charlie thought you might be engaged."

"Charlie thought wrong."

"But there must have been a reason he believed it possible," Mario insisted. "It is no secret you and Jack spent time together."

"Nothing's a secret around here," she said, throw-ing up her arms in despair. "So what if Jack and I dated a few times? Things didn't work out."

"Things didn't work out—what does that mean?"

"It means Jack and I are in two different places at this point in our lives. We're moving in different directions."

"Different places, different directions. That is nothing but foolish modern talk," he scoffed. "In my day, if a single man and an unmarried woman wanted to be together, nothing got in the way. I can't believe Jack let this happen."

"Sorry to break it to you, Dad, but men and women are equal participants these days."

"Okay, Miss Woman of the Nineties, don't you care for Jack?"

Care? If her father only knew. But the point was she didn't want him to know, or there'd be no end to this. "Dad, Jack and I were never engaged, we're not even dating now. We're—we're—friends. I'm sorry if that's not what you wanted, but that's the way it is."

"I never saw friends look at each other like that," he muttered, sitting back down.

"I beg your pardon?"

"At the party on Sunday, I saw the way Jack looked at you when he thought you didn't notice. And I saw the way you looked at him. You two should've been talking instead of giving each other all these looks."

"You must've imagined it."

"Like I imagined the look on your face when Jack offered Debbie Waslewski a ride home?"

As much as she disliked being reminded of that, Mary forced her voice to remain even. "That has nothing to do with me. Jack can give a ride to anybody he wants to."

With a sigh he reached for her hand. "Mary, sweetheart, I just want you to be happy, and if going to

Boston is what it takes, then so be it. Still, I have to tell you, I believe Jack coming back at this point in your life is a sign from God. You two may be too bull-headed to see it, but I am not."

His pale gray eyes were full of the concern and love she'd known all her life. If his words hadn't already made her teary, his gaze certainly would've finished the job. Yet fearing they'd only make things worse, she blinked the tears away. "All that sounds lovely, but it's not going to happen."

A stern look crossed his face. "Has Jack wronged you?"

"No, it's nothing like that. Believe me."

"Well, I hate to think I had been wrong about him again," he said, sounding relieved. He gave her hand a reassuring squeeze. "Isn't there something I can do? Talk to him, maybe?"

"We've already said all there is to say. There's nothing left."

"You're sure?"

"Yes." She patted the hand holding hers and then turned to the desk. She picked up the multipage contract. "This is what I want, Dad. And it will work out, you'll see."

"I hope so." He rose slowly from the chair. "You staying out here?"

"I need to keep reading. Call me when supper's ready?"

"Sure." He headed for the door, then paused midway to look back at her, shaking his head. "I can't believe there's nothing I can do for you and Jack."

"I'm a big girl now, remember? It's not up to you to do anything."

Her father didn't look convinced. With a silent shrug he left her to her reading. Yet she found it slow going, as her father's words kept sabotaging her concentration. He was a dear to want to set things right—what he thought was right—for her. He didn't, however, know the whole story. He didn't know that she'd been willing to figure out a way for her and Jack to be together, but Jack had refused. And he didn't know that she'd offered Jack her love, but that he'd refused that, too. No, her father, caring and giving man that he was, could never imagine that Jack had told her not to love him.

She was attempting to read clause seven for the second time when Peter Candelaria walked in through the office's front entrance. Clearly he was surprised to find her there.

"I came out here to read," she explained. "It's quieter than inside." Except it seemed like Grand Central Station right now.

"I'll be out of your way in a minute. I just came by to pick up keys for a house I'm showing tomorrow morning." He began rummaging through a drawer in his desk. "The owners refused to have a lockbox on their door."

"You're not in my way... it's your office."

After he'd found the key he wanted, he seemed hesitant to leave. Eventually he came over to where she was sitting. "Ah, Mary, I—I'm sorry for shooting my mouth off the night you came here. I shouldn't have talked that way to you."

"Forget it, Peter. I was pretty mouthy myself."

"Yeah, maybe. Still, everything you said was true. And I needed to hear it." He shoved his hand into his pants pocket. "I guess I really should thank you."

"If I helped, I'm glad," she said, shrugging. "Charlie told me you and Gina have patched things up."

"Yeah. I'm going to bring her and the kids home next week."

"Does that mean you and Jack are working things out?"

"We're talking, though nothing's decided. Going into business together is a big step, and I don't want to rush into anything. But, as long as I'm at least considering it, Gina's happy," he said. "And whether or not we become business partners, Jack and I are ready to be brothers again. Something you said made me see the light on that, too."

"What was that?"

"About traps being of our own making. And it's true, I trapped myself all these years by blaming Jack," he told her. "What incredible power I must've thought he had to keep me stuck in this rut. But it was my own doing all along."

"You've gotten past that now. That's what's important."

He rubbed the back of his neck with his hand. "Ah—I'd like to repay the favor," he added, after some hesitance. "Though I'm not sure how you'll feel about it."

"If this is what I think it's about, you can just save it, Peter. I just got an earful from my father about Jack, and I'm not in the mood for more."

"Fair enough. Still, I've got to tell you, Jack's unhappy you're leaving. Now, I don't know what really went on between you two, but maybe you're someone who should do some thinking about traps."

"You're right—you don't know what went on between us." Mary shuffled the contract back into the envelope. She had had just about enough for one day.

Marching out of the office, she swept through the house. "I'm not staying for supper after all," she informed her mother as she snatched up her purse.

"What?" Josephine looked at her as if she'd gone crazy. "But it's ready."

"Sorry, Mom," she called over her shoulder as she sailed out the back door. "I'm going home to get some peace and quiet."

Chapter Fourteen

After Mass the next day, Mary drove to her parents'
house in a calmer frame of mind. All she had needed
was a good night's sleep. Pushing aside the anxieties
surrounding her imminent departure, she wanted to
concentrate on enjoying a relaxed Sunday afternoon
with her family. She had even put off reviewing her
contract. Tonight she would reread it, sign it and have
it ready to mail first thing in the morning.

At the house her mother was sitting at the kitchen
table, reading the front page of the Sunday paper. "So
you're back," Josephine said, peering at Mary over
her bifocals. "You planning to stay long enough to eat
this time?"

"Sorry about that, Mom. But I was just bushed last
night."

"Likely story." She turned her attention back to the headlines, yet continued talking. "Your father said something to upset you, didn't he?"

"Did he tell you that?" Mary went to the stove to pour herself a cup of coffee.

"He hasn't told me anything. He clammed up with me last night, and he barely said two words to anybody after Mass this morning. That's not like him," Josephine insisted, holding out her empty cup for Mary to refill. "And now he's been on and off the phone, in and out of the office, driving off here and there."

"He probably has a house deal cooking."

"*Nonna, Nonna,* we're here!" Two little girls came barreling into the kitchen to become the immediate center of their grandmother's attention. There were hugs and kisses all around.

"Auntie Mary, you beat us here again," Jenny, the younger one, exclaimed. "Daddy said you drive too fast."

"Did he?"

"It's the truth." Charlie came in carrying various pieces of baby paraphernalia—diaper bag, infant seat, stroller. "You're going to get in all sorts of trouble with those crazy Boston drivers, you know."

Diane followed with the baby snuggled in her arms. "Don't mind him, Mary. Your brother's a sore loser."

"Tell me something I don't know," Mary quipped.

"I hate it when you women gang up on me." Charlie dropped the baby things by the door and then sniffed the aromas filling the kitchen. "Mmm . . . what's for dinner, Mom?"

"Risotto and sausage, and apple pie for dessert." Josephine folded up the newspaper before she got up from the table. "Since Mary has only a couple of more Sundays with us, I'm making her favorites each time. Next week, roast leg of lamb."

"Roast leg of lamb!" Charlie glared at Mary before breaking into a smile. He curved his arm around her shoulder in an affectionate squeeze. "You were always the princess around here."

Josephine held up her hand. "I'd do the same for you if you were moving away."

"Don't even think about it!" Diane added.

"Okay, all of you, out of my kitchen," Josephine commanded. "Mary, get the girls and have them help you set the table."

She winked at her brother, loving the familial camaraderie. "See. That's how far special treatment gets you around here."

Mary called her two older nieces into the dining room and handed them the table pad and cloth to spread out on the table. Watching as they took pains to smooth the white tablecloth just so, she felt an unexpected wistfulness. These girls had grown up before her eyes, each weekly family dinner providing an opportunity to see and measure the changes in them. And they were always such fun.

It certainly would be different, coming back only every month or so. The changes in the girls would not be subtle: she could leave one time with Lisa chattering about swim team and Girl Scouts, and then come back to find her niece oohing and ahhing over the latest rock 'n' roll heartthrob! She'd miss so much in between.

As they counted out the silverware and plates, the girls peppered her with questions about the new stores in Boston and where she was going to live.

"Will you be able to come to my First Communion next spring?" Jenny asked.

"Of course I will."

"And the second-grade holiday pageant?" Jenny added.

"I'm not so sure about that, honey. Depends on when it is."

Charlie came in with the baby's high chair. "Shall I put it in the usual spot?"

Mary had bought the high chair when Lisa was an infant, long before she'd been big enough to sit up in it. Today the chair reminded her of her oldest niece's first appearance at Sunday dinner. Less than two weeks old, she'd been a tiny fragile ball of warmth that everyone couldn't hold long enough—certainly not Auntie Mary. The first Piletti grandchild—they'd all been so excited. And each child thereafter had been greeted and loved with as much enthusiasm.

She gazed at Charlie setting up the pastel flowered high chair and the two little girls carefully placing forks and knives and spoons. Glancing at the place where she usually sat, she pictured Jack sitting beside her, eating, drinking and laughing with her family. And, perhaps, a child or two of their own sitting between them....

"Mary—Mary!"

She flinched, her little daydream shattering like glass before her eyes. She turned around to her father.

"Sweetheart, what's the matter? You were a million miles away."

"Not quite that far, Dad." She gave him a gentle smile, trying to read the expression on his face. "Are you upset about last night?"

"Last night? You mean our talk?" He shrugged as if the matter was of no consequence. "Ah, don't mind me. Thinking about you leaving got the better of me. But I understand. It's for the best."

"Really?"

"Yes, yes. Now let's speak no more about it," Mario insisted. "Besides, I want to know if you'd come see the Feeney house with me. You said you hadn't been inside it for years."

"Why are you going over there?"

Mario sighed and rolled his eyes. "How do I make a long story short?" he said. "Sally had me put it on the market a few weeks ago, and then she had second thoughts and had me take it off. Now she's changed her mind again."

"I thought Sally was vacationing in Florida," Charlie said, moving the high chair to the end of the table.

"She is. She found a condo she likes there and put a down payment on it. So this time the house stays on the market." Mario turned to her. "I thought you'd come help me look it over again, help me rethink the pricing."

"Gee, I'm not sure I'm in the mood for that today. Besides, I was planning on leaving early, I've got a lot of work to do at home." She decided it was better not to mention that this "work" included reviewing the business contract.

"Come on, sweetheart, it won't take long, and I sure could use your opinion." Mario gave her the kind of do-it-for-Papa look she hadn't seen in years. "Remember how you used to come preview houses with me when you were little?"

That got to her. Today was one day where sentiment worked like a charm. "When do you want to
go?"

"How about after dinner?"

Mary nodded in agreement as Jenny sidled up to
Mario. "Can we go look at the house, too, Grandpa?"

"Of course you can, my little sweetheart. The more
the merrier. Is that okay with you, son?" Mario
glanced at Charlie.

"Sorry guys, but didn't you hear me tell *Nonna* we
had to leave right after we eat?" Charlie asked the
girls. We're supposed to meet the O'Briens at their
church's fall fair."

"I forgot!" Jenny squealed. "Pony rides!"

The door from the kitchen swung open and Josephine entered, carrying a huge steaming platter of risotto. "Dinner's ready!"

"Sally's agreed to a complete exterior paint job. I
insisted," Mario said, as he pulled up to the big old
house. "The color's up to me. What do you think—
should we change it? Go with something more trendy?
Gray maybe?"

Mary was aghast. "But the Feeney house has always been yellow. It'd be like painting the White
House blue."

"Guess you're right. Yellow it stays."

Shivering against the late-October chill, she buttoned up her dark rose wool blazer as she followed her
father up the steps to the unscreened porch. She was
glad she'd changed out of the dress she'd worn to
church and into the warmer pair of jeans and the T-
shirt she kept in her car.

While Mario was busy with the door locks, she gazed out at the lawn, blanketed with a colorful multitude of fallen leaves. For the first time in years, she thought about the sheer giddy fun of jumping into a massive pile of freshly raked leaves. Somehow she wouldn't mind raking this expansive front lawn, if she had a couple of kids scampering about, ready to run and jump into the leaves when she gave the word. Maybe she would leap in right after them....

"I'd better hire someone to rake the yard," Mario muttered, holding the door open. "The prospect of raking all those leaves every fall could discourage a potential buyer."

Mary stepped inside. "Oh, Dad, I'd forgotten how wonderful this place is."

Roaming from room to room on the main floor, she marveled at the high ceilings and exquisite crown moldings, the spacious airiness of the rooms and the mellow wood floors. True, the place needed work, but the results would be well worth the effort.

"I've been trying to determine my marketing strategy for this time around," Mario said, as he led her through the kitchen. "I think I should aim it toward young couples with small children, or planning to have children. Couples with money—so fixing this place up won't seem too much of a big deal."

"It doesn't have to be that big of a deal."

"You don't think so?" Her father mulled this over a bit. "Well, it is a great family house. I'd like to see kids in it. Come on, I'll show you upstairs."

Walking up the distinctive front staircase, she stifled the urge to tell her father he'd better find a buyer who would appreciate and treasure this house as it should be. It'd sound too ridiculous. Yet she felt an inexplicable connection with this house—maybe because it was everything she thought a home should be. But that was ridiculous, as well. The house she'd grown up in was nothing like this.

"There are six bedrooms," Mario said, leading her through each one, ending with the sizable master bedroom. "That's a lot by today's standards. But this room connects to the smaller one next door." He opened a door in the back of the room. "See, that's the room we were just in."

Mary poked her head inside. "It was probably used for a nursery."

"I was thinking of pitching it as perfect for a large bathroom—turning this entire space into a master bedroom suite. They're real popular these days." He glanced around the small room. "This could easily fit his-and-her showers and a whirlpool tub. Wouldn't that be great?"

"I suppose so. Still, a young couple might want to keep it for a baby's room."

"It's sure getting chilly, isn't it?" her father said, zipping up his blue poplin jacket. "Wonder what shape the furnace is in. It's oil, and as old as the hills, I bet."

"You want to check it while we're here?"

"You wouldn't mind?" he asked, a quick smile lighting his face. "I mean, you sounded like you were in a hurry this afternoon."

"How long can it take? I'll come down to the basement and help you."

"No." Mario held up his hand. "You stay here and wait—see how warm these rooms get after I turn it on. That would be a big help."

He was out the door before she had a chance to agree. Actually she didn't mind waiting in this charming bedroom with its grand picture window overlooking the back lawns. Curling up on the chintz-covered window seat cushions, she contemplated why this house was affecting her so strongly. After all, it was a house she had visited only on occasion as a child. She didn't even know the Feeneys that well, so she had no real emotional connection with the house.

Yet, she *was* feeling connected.

"Admit it," she muttered to herself. "This is the kind of house you used to daydream about."

She gazed at the room before her, but her eyes weren't seeing the cabbage rose wallpaper nor the ornate fireplace. Instead, she saw herself cuddling with Jack in the large mahogany bed, murmuring to each other in the dark as the fire burned low... the door to the nursery was open a crack, in case the baby—their baby—cried for them in the night....

She forced herself to stop. What was going on with her? Earlier she had imagined having Jack beside her at her family's Sunday dinners, and now she was daydreaming about living in this house with him. Before, she'd simply dismissed the twinges of sadness and regret she'd been experiencing. She was, after all, making a major change in her life, leaving for something new and unknown. Wasn't it natural to feel a shade wistful? To wonder about what she might be leaving behind?

Except this time, sitting here in this house, these same questions brought different, unexpected answers.

Yes, it was natural to feel wistful and to wonder. But she was actually feeling something stronger by far, something daydreams could never satisfy. Suddenly, with a clarity that had evaded her for months, Mary could see the way ahead.

How could she have been so blind?

Fidgeting with new impatience, she glanced at her watch. Although the exact hour was unimportant, she prayed it wasn't too late.

Still, she wished her father would hurry up.

Mario Piletti was waiting for him on the front porch of the Feeney house, just as he'd said he would be.

He held out his hand as Jack approached. "Jackie, I'm glad you came, and you'll be glad, too," Mario said. "When Sally Feeney put the house back up for sale, you were the first person I thought to call. You really liked it when you saw it last time. Remember?"

Jack nodded. "I also remember saying it was too big."

"You might reconsider after you've seen it again," Mario said, holding the front door open for him. "Now that Sally's finally decided to move to Florida, I can negotiate some very attractive terms for you."

Jack walked inside the house, feeling sullen and out of sorts. He hadn't wanted to come back to this house today, and he certainly wasn't interested in buying it. This kind of big old family house was the last thing he needed. He could just see himself, alone, rambling through the empty rooms on cold, dark winter nights. Talk about depressing.

Sure, he had liked the house. Except that'd been back when his head was full of Mary, when the first blush of attraction and intrigue had just begun to take hold of his heart. He hadn't seriously considered buying it then, yet somewhere in the back of his mind...

Damn! He hadn't wanted to come back here. Yet the old man wouldn't take no for an answer. Mario had called him once last night and twice this morning, until he gave in. What else could he do? He knew Mario meant well.

As Mario led him from the front foyer into the living room, all the positive aspects of the place jumped out at him again: the spacious rooms, wood floors, high ceilings, solid plaster walls, beautiful windows. It was all there, everything as charming and attractive as before. Still, the fascination and excitement he had felt during his first visit was missing.

Trouble was, nothing much fascinated or excited him these days—not since he and Mary had decided to go their separate ways. Things only got worse after he'd brought the flowers to her store and learned she was in Boston renting an apartment. Even reconciling with Peter, great as it was, hadn't brought the joy he'd expected. Without Mary to share the highs and lows with, his days seemed to lose their edge. It was like his second reaction to this house: nothing felt right, and everything felt flat.

So much for getting on with his life!

Jack couldn't help thinking about the house in Lexington that he and Sandra had loved yet never had time to enjoy and eventually decided to discard. Just like their marriage. Yes, it was sad they hadn't tried harder to make their life together work. But how could they, when they'd been stuck in a pattern of all or nothing? And, true to his Candelaria genes, he'd been stuck in that pattern his entire life without realizing it. Until Mary.

All or nothing—the sure way to end up losing. Losing people. Losing love. Jack understood that now, and he wished Sandra had had the gift of time to learn this lesson, as well. But the hands of fate were unpredictable and never offered reasons for what they gave and took. Sandra was dead, while he'd been given a second chance to build his life. He had to accept that—accept it and make the most of it. The question now was how. The clock was ticking—soon Mary would be gone....

"Sure is getting chilly. Winter'll be here before you know it." Mario remarked, turning up his jacket collar. "Wonder what kind of shape the furnace is in. Maybe we should check."

Jack glanced at his watch. "Ah, Mario, I've got to get going."

"Won't take more than five or ten minutes."

Jack checked his watch again. Suddenly, time was crucial. Had he missed his chance?

"Would you mind?" Mario asked. "I could use a hand."

As he looked at the balding, gray-haired man he'd known all his life, Jack couldn't help thinking of his own father. In a fit of sentiment, he realized he could spare five minutes. "Okay. How do we get into the basement?"

Mario shook his head. "I'll go down to switch it on, and you go upstairs and see how long it takes for the heat to kick in. That'll give me an idea of what we're dealing with."

"If that's what you want."

"Just give a holler when you feel the heat," Mario said. Yet he had the oddest smile on his face as he disappeared around a corner.

*   *   *

Mary had been about to go hunt down her father when she heard his footsteps on the stairs. Finally! The heat never did come on, and she was beginning to wonder if he'd left without her. She sat back on the window seat and waited to tell him the dreary news. Repairing or replacing a furnace in a house this big and this old would be an expensive proposition, not one Sally Feeney or a prospective buyer would be eager to take on. Poor Dad.

Poor Dad seemed to be taking his sweet time walking down the hall. Her impatience multiplying, Mary reached for her purse and was about to head her father off at the pass when the dark handsome star of her current daydream appeared in the open doorway.

"Jack!" Her purse fell to the floor.

"Mary? What are you doing here?"

She was stunned. "What are *you* doing here?"

"I'm looking at the house with your father."

"So am I."

His eyes narrowed. "He told me to come upstairs and holler when the heat kicks in."

"Did he?" Suddenly she realized what was going on, and her initial shock gave way to disbelief. Where did her father get off pulling a trick like this? She headed for the door. "He's gonna hear hollering all right."

But then she heard a car start up outside.

"Oh, no." She dashed across the hall to a front bedroom with Jack right behind her. They both got to a window in time to see her father driving merrily away.

"Of all the damn fool stunts," Jack muttered.

"I don't know what he hoped to accomplish." She stared out the window until her father's car rolled out of sight, trying hard to keep a rein on her own anger.

"Don't you?"

As she turned around to Jack, her thoughts froze. She felt awkward, despite the romantic scenes of reconciliation that had been running through her mind while she'd waited for her father. Or because of them. Jack looked rather uncomfortable, himself. Obviously she was the last person he wanted to be "trapped" with. What had she been thinking?

"I've got to get my purse."

Jack followed her back into the master bedroom. "I'll drive you home."

"Thanks, but I can walk to my folks' house," she said, stooping in front of the window seat to pick her handbag off the floor. "I've got a thing or two to say to my father, anyway."

Turning to say goodbye, she was startled by the mirth twinkling in Jack's eyes.

"Your old man snookered us good, didn't he?" His lips curved into a slow smile.

She couldn't help smiling back. "What a performance! It'd never occurred to me he was pulling a fast one. 'Wonder what shape the furnace is in,' " Mary quoted in a voice that quavered until she gave in to the laugh bubbling inside of her.

Jack began laughing, too, and they spurred each other on. She didn't care. Laughter was a welcome relief from the tension racking the air between them. Besides, it felt so good to laugh like this—to let herself go—to share something with Jack once more.

Still, when the laughter eventually died out, the tension remained. And in the ensuing silence Mary felt it more keenly. He was so close she could feel the heat from his body, and she longed to reach out to feel this warmth beneath her hand. Her lover...her best friend. They might never be alone like this again, never be standing this close. The pain of this thought was almost too much to bear, and she was torn between running to him and running away.

Her heart in turmoil, she turned to him, praying she'd find the right words. But the look in his eyes took her breath away. The warm chocolate gaze she'd come to adore was unwavering, burning with an intensity that made her knees weak. She really loved this man.

"Dammit...Mary...this is ridiculous. We should be together." His voice cracking with emotion, Jack opened his arms out to her.

She whispered his name as his arms circled around her, pulling her hard against his taut chest. For weeks she had secretly yearned to be held like this again, to be wrapped in his strength, to feel the powerful beat of his heart.

"I love you, Mary. So much," he murmured in her ear, his hands caressing her back. "I can't lose you—not now."

"I love you, too." Fighting back tears, she pressed deeper into his embrace.

"Baby, I want you any way I can have you. Anywhere. I'll go to Boston with you, if that's what it takes."

Stunned, she pulled back. "You mean that?" she asked, peering up at him. "You'd give up Springfield? Everything you came home for?"

"Say the word and I'll leave with you tonight," he said, holding her like he'd never let her go. "Because my life here isn't going to work without you."

"I—I don't understand. You wanted this so much."

"I must've told you a dozen times how empty my life in Boston was, how lonely... but it's ten times worse here without you." Easing his embrace, he sought her gaze. "What we have together is a once-in-a-lifetime thing—you just don't throw that away. Mary, you've got to believe I love you, that I need to be wherever you are."

Believe him? All she had to do was think of the progress Jack had made in Springfield—with his business, with the neighborhood and most of all with his brother—to realize that the man who'd never made a sacrifice for anyone was willing to make the supreme one for her. For her.

Feeling truly lovestruck, she wanted nothing more than to lose herself in the smoldering depths of his eyes. They drew her to him like a magnet. Cupping his face with her hands, she moved closer until their lips met and she kissed him with a passion too long locked away.

"Jack," she breathed against his cheek after they finally let each other go. "Jack, we don't have to pack up lock, stock and barrel and move to Boston to be together."

He held her away from him. "But Boston is what you wanted."

"And I want a life—here—with you, too. It's been haunting me all weekend. I can't focus. I get distracted. I haven't even been able to read my partnership contract, never mind sign it."

"What happened?"

"My father... this house... your brother."

Jack looked surprised. "What did Peter have to do with it?"

"Reminded me of this great little speech I made to him about traps being of our own making. He told me I should give some thought to traps, myself," she explained. "And he was right. I finally understood that since you came into my life, I've felt less and less trapped. Now, why should we trap ourselves into one corner or the other? We're two, bright, motivated people. We can work something out. That is, if you're willing...."

"You bet I'm willing." Jack smiled down at her, his gaze warming her like a velvet caress. "Sweetheart, thanks to you I'm learning the beauty of compromise. Now I understand how. If we hold tight to each other, we'll find a way to get the best of Springfield and Boston."

Mary rested her head against his chest, holding on to him tight. "The moment you walked into this room, I knew why I'd been putting off signing those papers. I love you—I have since that day I watched you help the little girl pick out her first bicycle. Remember? I ran out of the store before you saw me?"

"How could I forget? I went crazy trying to find you afterward," he added. "That was the same afternoon we made love for the first time. Remember?"

"I'll never forget." She snuggled closer.

Jack pressed a kiss on the top of her head. "You like this house?"

"Love it," she murmured. "Always have. And you?"

"I haven't been able to get it out of my mind since your father first showed it to me weeks ago. Every house I've seen since has paled in comparison."

"Then why didn't you buy it?"

"Because I didn't have you."

She met his gaze, finding it warm, sexy, brimming with love. Gazing deeper, she saw her own reflection and knew, without a doubt, she was where she belonged.

"Mary, let's make this house part of the life we build together—the part that means kids and friends and family." His voice was husky and low, and the love in his eyes delved deep into her soul. "Please, please marry me."

"I will, Jack," she whispered without the slightest hesitancy. "There's no place else on earth I want to be."

He pulled her close again, his mouth seeking hers. Jack's kiss was unrelenting, dizzying, wonderful. She could practically taste his pent-up love and desire pouring into her and it was glorious.

When he released her lips at last, his arms stayed firmly around her. "We're going to have a wonderful life together, Mary. I promise."

"There's not a doubt in my mind."

He smiled, shaking his head. "When I think of the shape I was in when I first came back, this seems almost too good to be true. My marriage had failed. My brother hated me. People around here wouldn't give me the time of day. Coming home had begun to look like a huge mistake," Jack admitted. "Then I found you and everything began to feel right. When I fell in love with you, I belonged again."

"With or without me, Jack, you belong here. Your family needs you."

"After twenty years and a lot of grief," he said, shrugging. "But everything that's happened in my life—good and bad—has taught me what a lucky fool I am to have found you. Coming home was the smartest move I ever made."

Mary planted a kiss on his cheek. "Welcome home."

He smiled into her eyes. "Speaking of home, there's a real estate agent I need to talk to about a house. He mentioned something about attractive terms."

"I happen to have excellent family connections in that department," she said with a knowing wink. "But we should demand a guarantee that the furnace works."

"I can't wait to see the look on your father's face."

"Neither can I."

"Shall we?" Jack held out his hand.

Thinking ahead to the years of loving nights she and Jack would spend there, Mary gave the master bedroom one last look. "We'll be back," she whispered.

Hand in hand she and Jack left the house that, one day soon, would be their home. Gratified victims of her father's crafty hoax, they drove off to surprise him with the news that he'd just made the sale of a lifetime.

Epilogue

It was a perfect June day, and a perfect day of rejoicing for the Piletti and Candelaria families. Mary and Jack exchanged marriage vows at St. Camille's in a ceremony laced with laughter and joyous tears. The church was packed with family, friends and neighbors. By the time she and Jack had greeted every last guest in the receiving line following the ceremony, they were more than ready to celebrate.

And what a party Mario and Josephine Piletti had planned!

Mary looked about the vast reception hall as the band played, guests danced, wine flowed and the food was plentiful. All of Peek Street was there, and what seemed like half of Springfield. This was the typical big, fancy Italian wedding she'd thought she was too old for at first. Now she was glad she'd agreed to it. Not only had it made her parents and Rose Candelaria happy, but the months and weeks of planning and preparation had been fun for both her and Jack. And right now, she and her groom were having a grand time greeting guests and dancing.

"Although I'd much rather dance with you again, Mrs. Candelaria," Jack murmured in her ear after a particularly romantic slow dance, "both our mothers are madly waving at us to come over."

Mary followed Jack's gaze to find Josephine and Rose, in their colorful mother-of-the-bride and mother-of-the-groom ensembles, hovering at a corner guest table. "That's my mother's cousin Elio and his wife. They came all the way from Florida."

"Mary must have tried on a dozen gowns before we found this one," her mother was saying as they approached the table.

"Then we go to Filene's in Boston, and the first one she tries on is perfect, just perfect," Rose added, glancing at Mary. "Doesn't she make a beautiful bride?"

"Absolutely," Jack interjected, much to everyone's delight. And when he looked at her with that appreciative gleam in his deep dark eyes, she felt beautiful.

Upon leaving these relatives, Mary led Jack to where Lorna and Terry Michael were seated with their respective mates. She was so glad they'd been able to come out for the wedding. Her decision to renegotiate her contract to become a consulting partner in their new business had worked out better than Mary could've hoped, and the three of them had grown closer in the past months. Although she was not involved in the day-to-day running of the Boston shops, she worked closely with the Michaels on all aspects of planning and operations via phone, fax, computer and regular trips into town.

"Oh, Mary, the ceremony was just lovely," Lorna declared, greeting her with a warm hug. "And you look gorgeous!"

"The big guy looks pretty good, too," Terry playfully threaded her arm through Jack's, sending a wink Mary's way.

Mary smiled, happy that Jack got along with her business partners. They'd come to know him well because he often accompanied Mary on her minitrips to Boston—staying at the cozy apartment he had encouraged her to keep even after her original plans had changed.

After visiting with the Michaels, Mary and Jack were sidetracked by Diane and Charlie.

"Okay, guys, I've got your car all tanked up and ready to go," her brother announced. "It's parked right out front here."

"No silly decorations, right?" Mary warned.

"Would I do anything so childish?" Charlie asked with mock innocence. "Of course, I can't be responsible for what some of the other pranksters around here might do."

"Lisa and Jenny did insist on a Just Married sign," Diane offered. "I knew you wouldn't mind that."

"Of course not." Mary smiled at her sister-in-law, who looked radiant in her summer green matron-of-honor gown. "However, knowing my brother's penchant for wedding-day tricks, I'm a little concerned."

"Don't worry, I've been watching him like a hawk," Diane said.

"That's the truth," Charlie agreed, turning to hook a friendly arm around Jack's shoulder. "Now, pal, we all know you two are leaving on a flight to Bermuda tomorrow. But you haven't told us where you'll be tonight.''

"That's private, pal.''

Jack glanced her way. His smoky gaze reminded her he'd arranged to have champagne on ice waiting for them in the newly redecorated master bedroom of their big yellow house. They had both agreed they'd rather spend their wedding night there than in a hotel.

"Smart move, Jack. Why invite trouble from people who should know better?'' Diane added with a pointed glare at her husband. Then she put her hand on Mary's arm. "I don't want you worrying about Twice as Nice. Gina and I will keep everything under control while you're away.''

"I hope I'm not dumping too much on you two, what with all the summer stuff coming in.''

Diane waved off Mary's concern. "Are you kidding? We're going to have a blast because Rose and your parents have offered to watch all the kids—all day long.''

"They have? That's great. But where is my father, anyway?'' Mary wondered aloud.

Jack shook his head. "I haven't seen him since he danced with Aunt Angie.''

Charlie laughed. "Last time I saw Dad he was over at the bar with the New York cousins, boasting how he finally got you two together.''

"And sold a house in the bargain,'' Mary added with a knowing grin.

Everyone knew the story. Mario had told it to anyone who'd asked and to some who hadn't. The news had zoomed through the neighborhood grapevine with a speed that'd amazed even her. Yet, the congratulations and best wishes offered by the neighbors had been genuine and heartfelt. People were really very happy for her and Jack. No matter how much tongues had wagged over the years about this crisis or that embarrassment, everyone on Peek Street loved a happy ending.

Mary and Jack moved on to mingle with more guests until they eventually came across her father at the very back of the reception hall, sipping brandy and passing time with his lifelong pal, Dickie Ladero. Dickie shook Jack's hand and kissed Mary on the cheek.

"Beautiful wedding, just beautiful. Even your old man got choked up during the ceremony," Dickie said, giving his old buddy a gentle elbow in the ribs. "Didn't know I caught that, eh, Mario?"

Her father waved Dickie off. "Just wait till you walk your only daughter down the aisle."

When Dickie excused himself to rejoin his wife, her father insisted she and Jack sit down with him. "I have something to say to you two, so I better do it before people start dragging you away again." He looked sternly at Jack. "You, young man, better take good care of my daughter. Work hard for her—treat her right. And if you don't... you'll have to answer to me."

"I love Mary more than life itself, sir, and I'll do everything in my power to make our life together the best it can be. I promise you," Jack said, melting her heart with his words.

"Good, good." Nodding his approval, her father then turned to her. "And the same goes for you, young lady. You've got yourself a fine man here. Be a good wife to him.''

His gruff voice belied the tear welling up in his eye, and Mary leaned closer to kiss his cheek. "I will, Dad. I promise.''

"Fine. That's what I want to hear. Now, I have one piece of good-old-fashioned advice," her father said, using his gruffness as a cover while he quickly composed himself. "Never go to bed angry."

She couldn't keep from chuckling. "Mama said the exact same thing to me this morning."

Her father laughed, too. "After thirty-six years of marriage, we should know."

A waiter, carrying two glasses of champagne on a tray, approached the table. "Mr. and Mrs. Candelaria, the best man is about to deliver the toast," he announced, offering them the champagne.

With glasses in hand, they wound their way through the crowd to the front of the room as the band finished playing, and Peter began his toast to the bride and groom.

"In my wildest dreams, I never imagined I'd be standing here, giving a toast at my brother's wedding," Peter began, his eyes seeking Jack out in the crowd. He smiled when he found him. "But I'm so honored to be doing just that. We've come a long way in a short time, haven't we, Jack?''

Mary watched Jack grin broadly as he nodded and gave Peter the thumbs-up sign. This warm relationship with his brother was something Jack had wanted for so long—it thrilled her to see the pleasure it gave him.

"After too many years, I've found both a supportive brother and a helluva friend, for which I am grateful," Peter continued. "And I could go on and on about Jack's innumerable qualities, but the fact that he's the man who finally won our fair Mary says it all for me.

"And, Mary," he said, catching her eye. "We're all grateful you didn't leave Springfield in the end, for the loss would not only have been Jack's. You've been a good friend to all of us over the years, and you deserve only the best.

"So please join me in wishing Jack and Mary luck and happiness." Peter lifted his glass to them. "May you always have love wherever you are, wherever you go, and may the home you make together be full of laughter and joy."

As more than a hundred clinking glasses chimed around them, Mary and Jack looked deep into each other's eyes. They knew Peter's wish for them was already a dream come true.

* * * * *

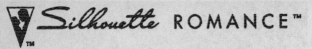

Silhouette ROMANCE™

**First comes marriage.... Will love follow?
Find out this September when Silhouette Romance
presents**

Join six couples who marry for convenient reasons, and still find happily-ever-afters. Look for these wonderful books by some of your favorite authors:

#1030 *Timely Matrimony* by Kasey Michaels
#1031 *McCullough's Bride* by Anne Peters
#1032 *One of a Kind Marriage* by Cathie Linz
#1033 *Oh, Baby!* by Lauryn Chandler
#1034 *Temporary Groom* by Jayne Addison
#1035 *Wife in Name Only* by Carolyn Zane

by Christine Rimmer

Three rapscallion brothers. Their main talent: making trouble. Their only hope: three uncommon women who knew the way to heal a wounded heart! Meet them in these books:

Jared Jones

hadn't had it easy with women. Retreating to his mountain cabin, he found willful Eden Parker waiting to show him a good woman's love in MAN OF THE MOUNTAIN (May, SE #886).

Patrick Jones

was determined to show Regina Black that a wild Jones boy was *not* husband material. But that wouldn't stop her from trying to nab him in SWEETBRIAR SUMMIT (July, SE #896)!

Jack Roper

came to town looking for the wayward and beautiful Olivia Larrabee. He never suspected he'd uncover a long-buried Jones family secret in A HOME FOR THE HUNTER (September, SE #908)....

Meet these rascal men and the women who'll tame them, only from Silhouette Books and Special Edition!

Premiere

The stars are out in October at Silhouette! Read
captivating love stories by talented *new* authors—
in their very first Silhouette appearance.

Sizzle with Susan Crosby's
THE MATING GAME—Desire #888
...when Iain Mackenzie and Kani Warner are forced
to spend their days—and *nights*—together in *very* close
tropical quarters!

Explore the passion in Sandra Moore's
HIGH COUNTRY COWBOY—Special Edition #918
...where Jake Valiteros tries to control the demons that
haunt him—along with a stubborn woman as wild as the
Wyoming wind.

Cherish the emotion in Kia Cochrane's
MARRIED BY A THREAD—Intimate Moments #600
...as Dusty McKay tries to recapture the love he once
shared with his wife, Tori.

Exhilarate in the power of Christie Clark's
TWO HEARTS TOO LATE—Romance #1041
...as Kirby Anne Gordon and Carl Tannon fight for custody
of a small child...and battle their growing attraction!

Shiver with Val Daniels'
BETWEEN DUSK AND DAWN—Shadows #42
...when a mysterious stranger claims to want to save
Jonna Sanders from a serial killer.

Catch the classics of tomorrow—*premiering* today—
Only from

V Silhouette®

PREM94